THE ROAD TO THE STARS

HOUGHTON MIFFLIN COMPANY BOSTON

Atlanta Dallas Geneva, Illinois Palo Alto Princeton Toronto

Cover Illustration Rudy Gutierrez

Printed in the U.S.A.

0-395-61874-6

123456789-B-96 95 94 93 92

Contents

The Million-Year Picnic

by Ray Bradbury

October 2026

Somehow the idea was brought up by Mom that perhaps the whole family would enjoy a fishing trip. But they weren't Mom's words; Timothy knew that. They were Dad's words, and Mom used them for him somehow.

Dad shuffled his feet in a clutter of Martian pebbles and agreed. So immediately there was a tumult and a shouting, and very quickly the camp was tucked into capsules and containers, Mom slipped into traveling jumpers and blouse, Dad stuffed his pipe full with trembling hands, his eyes on the Martian sky, and the three boys piled yelling into the motorboat, none of them really keeping an eye on Mom and Dad, except Timothy.

Dad pushed a stud. The water boat sent a humming sound up into the sky. The water shook back and the boat nosed ahead, and the family cried, 'Hurrah!'

Timothy sat in the back of the boat with Dad, his small fingers atop Dad's hairy ones, watching the canal twist, leaving the crumbled place behind where they had landed in their small family rocket all the way from Earth. He remembered the night before they left Earth, the hustling and hurrying, the rocket that Dad had found somewhere, somehow, and the talk of a vacation on Mars. A long way to go for a vacation, but Timothy said nothing because of his younger brothers. They came to Mars and now, first thing, or so they said, they were going fishing.

Dad had a funny look in his eyes as the boat went up-canal. A look that Timothy couldn't figure. It was made of strong light and maybe a sort of relief. It made the deep wrinkles laugh instead of worry or cry.

So there went the cooling rocket, around a bend, gone.

'How far are we going?' Robert splashed his hand. It looked like a small crab jumping in the violet water.

Dad exhaled. 'A million years.'

'Gee,' said Robert.

'Look, kids.' Mother pointed one soft long arm. 'There's a dead city.'

They looked with fervent anticipation, and the dead city lay dead for them alone, drowsing in a hot silence of summer made on Mars by a Martian weatherman.

And Dad looked as if he was pleased that it was dead.

It was a futile spread of pink rocks sleeping on a rise of sand, a few tumbled pillars, one lonely shrine, and then the sweep of sand again. Nothing else for miles. A white desert around the canal and a blue desert over it.

Just then a bird flew up. Like a stone thrown across a blue pond, hitting, falling deep, and vanishing.

Dad got a frightened look when he saw it. 'I thought it was a rocket.'

Timothy looked at the deep ocean sky, trying to see Earth and the war and the ruined cities and the men killing each other since the day he was born. But he saw nothing. The war was as removed and far off as two flies battling to the death in the arch of a great high and silent cathedral. And just as senseless.

William Thomas wiped his forehead and felt the touch of his son's hand on his arm, like a young tarantula, thrilled. He beamed at his son. 'How goes it, Timmy?'

'Fine, Dad.'

Timothy hadn't quite figured out what was ticking inside the vast adult mechanism beside him. The man with the immense hawk nose, sunburnt, peeling—and the hot blue eyes like agate marbles you play with after school in summer back on Earth, and the long thick columnar legs in the loose riding breeches.

'What are you looking at so hard, Dad?'

'I was looking for Earthian logic, common sense, good government, peace, and responsibility.'

'All that up there?'

'No. I didn't find it. It's not there any more. Maybe it'll never be there again. Maybe we fooled ourselves that it was ever there.'

'Huh?'

'See the fish,' said Dad, pointing.

There rose a soprano clamor from all three boys as they rocked the boat in arching their tender necks to see. They *oohed* and *ahed.* A silver ring fish floated by them, undulating, and closing like an iris, instantly, around food particles, to assimilate them.

Dad looked at it. His voice was deep and quiet.

'Just like war. War swims along, sees food, contracts. A moment later—Earth is gone.'

'William,' said Mom.

'Sorry,' said Dad.

They sat still and felt the canal water rush cool, swift, and glassy. The only sound was the motor hum, the glide of water, the sun expanding the air.

'When do we see the Martians?' cried Michael.

'Quite soon, perhaps,' said Father. 'Maybe tonight.'

'Oh, but the Martians are a dead race now,' said Mom.

'No, they're not. I'll show you some Martians, all right,' Dad said presently.

Timothy scowled at that but said nothing. Everything was odd now. Vacations and fishing and looks between people.

The other boys were already engaged making shelves of their small hands and peering under them toward the seven-foot stone banks of the canal, watching for Martians.

'What do they look like?' demanded Michael.

'You'll know them when you see them.' Dad sort of laughed, and Timothy saw a pulse beating time in his cheek.

Mother was slender and soft, with a woven plait of spun-gold hair over her head in a tiara, and eyes the color of the deep cool canal water where it ran in shadow, almost purple, with flecks of amber caught in it. You could see her thoughts swimming around in her eyes, like fish—some bright, some dark, some fast, quick, some slow and easy, and sometimes, like when she looked up where Earth was, being nothing but color and nothing else. She sat in the boat's prow, one hand resting on the side lip, the other on the lap of her dark breeches, and a line of sunburnt soft neck showing where her blouse opened like a white flower.

She kept looking ahead to see what was there, and, not being able to see it clearly enough, she looked backward toward her husband, and through his eyes, reflected then, she saw what was ahead; and since he added part of himself to this reflection, a determined firmness, her face relaxed and she accepted it and she turned back, knowing suddenly what to look for.

Timothy looked too. But all he saw was a straight pencil line of canal going violet through a wide shallow valley penned by low, eroded hills, and on until it fell over the sky's edge. And this canal went on and on, through cities that would have rattled like beetles in a dry skull if you shook them. A hundred or two hundred cities dreaming hot summer-day dreams and cold summer-night dreams . . .

They had come millions of miles for this outing—to fish. But there had been a gun on the rocket. This was a vacation. But why all the food, more than enough to last them years and years, left hidden back there near the rocket? Vacation. Just behind the veil of the vacation was not a soft face of laughter, but something hard and bony and perhaps terrifying. Timothy could not lift the veil, and the two other boys were busy being ten and eight years old, respectively.

'No Martians yet. Nuts.' Robert put his V-shaped chin on his hands and glared at the canal.

Dad had brought an atomic radio along, strapped to his wrist. It functioned on an old-fashioned principle: you held it against the bones near your ear and it vibrated singing or talking to you. Dad listened to it now. His face looked like one of those fallen Martian cities, caved in, sucked dry, almost dead.

Then he gave it to Mom to listen. Her lips dropped open.

'What—' Timothy started to question, but never finished what he wished to say.

For at that moment there were two titanic, marrow-jolting explosions that grew upon themselves, followed by a half dozen minor concussions.

Jerking his head up, Dad notched the boat speed higher immediately. The boat leaped and jounced and spanked. This shook Robert out of his funk and elicited yelps of frightened but ecstatic joy from Michael, who clung to Mom's legs and watched the water pour by his nose in a wet torrent.

Dad swerved the boat, cut speed, and ducked the craft into a little branch canal and under an ancient, crumbling stone wharf that smelled of crab flesh. The boat rammed the wharf hard enough to throw them all forward, but no one was hurt, and Dad was already twisted to see if the ripples on the canal were enough to map their route into hiding. Water lines went across, lapped the stones, and rippled back to meet each other, settling, to be dappled by the sun. It all went away.

Dad listened. So did everybody.

Dad's breathing echoed like fists beating against the cold wet wharf stones. In the shadow, Mom's cat eyes just watched Father for some clue to what next.

Dad relaxed and blew out a breath, laughing at himself.

'The rocket, of course. I'm getting jumpy. The rocket.'

Michael said, 'What happened, Dad, what happened?'

'Oh, we just blew up our rocket, is all,' said Timothy, trying to sound matter-of-fact. 'I've heard rockets blown up before. Ours just blew.'

'Why did we blow up our rocket?' asked Michael. 'Huh, Dad?'

'It's part of the game, silly!' said Timothy.

'A game!' Michael and Robert loved the word.

'Dad fixed it so it would blow up and no one'd know where we landed or went! In case they ever came looking, see?'

'Oh boy, a secret!'

'Scared by my own rocket,' admitted Dad to Mom. 'I *am* nervous. It's silly to think there'll ever be any more rockets. Except *one,* perhaps, if Edwards and his wife get through with *their* ship.'

He put his tiny radio to his ear again. After two minutes he dropped his hand as you would drop a rag.

'It's over at last,' he said to Mom. 'The radio just went off the atomic beam. Every other world station's gone. They dwindled down to a couple in the last few years. Now the air's completely silent. It'll probably remain silent.'

'For how long?' asked Robert.

'Maybe—your great-grandchildren will hear it again,' said Dad. He just sat there, and the children were caught in the center of his awe and defeat and resignation and acceptance.

Finally he put the boat out into the canal again, and they continued in the direction in which they had originally started.

It was getting late. Already the sun was down the sky, and a series of dead cities lay ahead of them.

Dad talked very quietly and gently to his sons. Many times in the past he had been brisk, distant, removed from them, but now he patted them on the head with just a word and they felt it.

'Mike, pick a city.'

'What, Dad?'

'Pick a city, Son. Any one of these cities we pass.'

'All right,' said Michael. 'How do I pick?'

'Pick the one you like the most. You, too, Robert and Tim. Pick the city you like best.'

'I want a city with Martians in it,' said Michael.

'You'll have that,' said Dad. 'I promise.' His lips were for the children, but his eyes were for Mom.

They passed six cities in twenty minutes. Dad didn't say anything more about the explosions; he seemed much more interested in having fun with his sons, keeping them happy, than anything else.

Michael liked the first city they passed, but this was vetoed because everyone doubted quick first judgments. The second city nobody liked. It was an Earth Man's settlement, built of wood and already rotting into sawdust. Timothy liked the third city because it was large. The fourth and fifth were too small and the sixth brought acclaim from everyone, including Mother, who joined in the Gees, Goshes, and Look-at-thats!

There were fifty or sixty huge structures still standing, streets were dusty but paved, and you could see one or two old centrifugal fountains still pulsing wetly in the plazas. That was the only life—water leaping in the late sunlight.

'This is the city,' said everybody.

Steering the boat to a wharf, Dad jumped out.

'Here we are. This is ours. This is where we live from now on!'

'From now on?' Michael was incredulous. He stood up, looking, and then turned to blink back at where the rocket used to be. 'What about the rocket? What about Minnesota?'

'Here,' said Dad.

He touched the small radio to Michael's blond head. 'Listen.'

Michael listened.

'Nothing,' he said.

'That's right. Nothing. Nothing at all any more. No more Minneapolis, no more rockets, no more Earth.'

Michael considered the lethal revelation and began to sob little dry sobs.

'Wait a moment,' said Dad the next instant. 'I'm giving you a lot more in exchange, Mike!'

'What?' Michael held off the tears, curious, but quite ready to continue in case Dad's further revelation was as disconcerting as the original.

'I'm giving you this city, Mike. It's yours.'

'Mine?'

'For you and Robert and Timothy, all three of you, to own for yourselves.'

Timothy bounded from the boat. 'Look, guys, all for *us*! All of *that*!' He was playing the game with Dad, playing it large and playing it well. Later, after it was all over and things had settled, he could go off by himself and cry for ten minutes. But now it was still a game, still a family outing, and the other kids must be kept playing.

Mike jumped out with Robert. They helped Mom.

'Be careful of your sister,' said Dad, and nobody knew what he meant until later.

They hurried into the great pink-stoned city, whispering among themselves, because dead cities have a way of making you want to whisper, to watch the sun go down.

'In about five days,' said Dad quietly, 'I'll go back down to where our rocket was and collect the food hidden in the ruins there and bring it here; and I'll hunt for Bert Edwards and his wife and daughters there.'

'Daughters?' asked Timothy. 'How many?'

'Four.'

'I can see that'll cause trouble later.' Mom nodded slowly.

'Girls.' Michael made a face with an ancient Martian stone image. 'Girls.'

'Are they coming in a rocket too?'

'Yes. If they make it. Family rockets are made for travel to the Moon, not Mars. We were lucky we got through.'

'Where did you get the rocket?' whispered Timothy, for the other boys were running ahead.

'I saved it. I saved it for twenty years, Tim. I had it hidden away, hoping I'd never have to use it. I suppose I should have given it to the government for the war, but I kept thinking about Mars. . . .'

'And a picnic!'

'Right. This is between you and me. When I saw everything was finishing on Earth, after I'd waited until the last moment, I packed us up. Bert Edwards had a ship hidden, too, but we decided it would be safer to take off separately, in case anyone tried to shoot us down.'

'Why'd you blow up the rocket, Dad?'

'So we can't go back, ever. And so if any of those evil men ever come to Mars they won't know we're here.'

'Is that why you look up all the time?'

'Yes, it's silly. They won't follow us, ever. They haven't anything to follow with. I'm being too careful, is all.'

Michael came running back. 'Is this really *our* city, Dad?'

'The whole darn planet belongs to us, kids. The whole darn planet.'

They stood there, King of the Hill, Top of the Heap, Ruler of All They Surveyed, Unimpeachable Monarchs and Presidents, trying to understand what it meant to own a world and how big a world really was.

Night came quickly in the thin atmosphere, and Dad left them in the square by the pulsing fountain, went down to the boat, and came walking back carrying a stack of paper in his big hands.

He laid the papers in a clutter in an old courtyard and set them afire. To keep warm, they crouched around the blaze and laughed, and Timothy saw the little letters leap like frightened animals when the flames touched and engulfed them. The papers crinkled like an old man's skin, and the cremation surrounded innumerable words:

'GOVERNMENT BONDS; Business Graph, 1999; Religious Prejudice: An Essay; The Science of Logistics; Problems of the Pan-American Unity; Stock Report for July 3, 1998; The War Digest . . .'

Dad had insisted on bringing these papers for this purpose. He sat there and fed them into the fire, one by one, with satisfaction, and told his children what it all meant.

'It's time I told you a few things. I don't suppose it was fair, keeping so much from you. I don't know if you'll understand, but I have to talk, even if only part of it gets over to you.'

He dropped a leaf in the fire.

'I'm burning a way of life, just like the way of life is being burned clean of Earth right now. Forgive me if I talk like a politician. I am, after all, a former state governor, and I was honest and they hated me for it. Life on Earth never settled down to doing anything very good. Science ran too far ahead of us too quickly, and the people got lost in a mechanical wilderness, like children making over pretty things, gadgets, helicopters, rockets; emphasizing the wrong items, emphasizing machines instead of how to run the machines. Wars got bigger and bigger and finally killed Earth. That's what the silent radio means. That's what we ran away from.

'We were lucky. There aren't any more rockets left. It's time you knew this isn't a fishing trip at all. I put off telling you. Earth is gone. Interplanetary travel won't be back for centuries, maybe never. But that way of life proved itself wrong and strangled itself with its own hands. You're young. I'll tell you this again every day until it sinks in.'

He paused to feed more papers to the fire.

'Now we're alone. We and a handful of others who'll land in a few days. Enough to start over. Enough to turn away from all that back on Earth and strike out on a new line—'

The fire leaped up to emphasize his talking. And then all the papers were gone except one. All the laws and beliefs of Earth were burnt into small hot ashes which soon would be carried off in a wind.

Timothy looked at the last thing that Dad tossed in the fire. It was a map of the World, and it wrinkled and distorted itself hotly and went—flimpf—and was gone like a warm, black butterfly. Timothy turned away.

'Now I'm going to show you the Martians,' said Dad. 'Come on, all of you. Here, Alice.' He took her hand.

Michael was crying loudly, and Dad picked him up and carried him, and they walked down through the ruins toward the canal.

The canal. Where tomorrow or the next day their future wives would come up in a boat, small laughing girls now, with their father and mother.

The night came down around them, and there were stars. But Timothy couldn't find Earth. It had already set. That was something to think about.

A night bird called among the ruins as they walked. Dad said, 'Your mother and I will try to teach you. Perhaps we'll fail. I hope not. We've had a good lot to see and learn from. We planned this trip years ago, before you were born. Even if there hadn't been a war we would have come to Mars, I think, to live and form our own standard of living. It would have been another century before Mars would have been really poisoned by the Earth civilization. Now, of course—'

They reached the canal. It was long and straight and cool and wet and reflective in the night.

'I've always wanted to see a Martian,' said Michael. 'Where are they, Dad? You promised.'

'There they are,' said Dad, and he shifted Michael on his shoulder and pointed straight down.

The Martians were there. Timothy began to shiver.

The Martians were there—in the canal—reflected in the water. Timothy and Michael and Robert and Mom and Dad.

The Martians stared back up at them for a long, long silent time from the rippling water. . . .

Little Green Men

by Barry B. Longyear

JHANNI caught his breath and rested in the shade of a boulder; he had found nothing. His father had forbidden him to search with the other Star Scouts for the UFO reported three days ago, and he wouldn't think of disobeying his father. Still, I said nothing about searching on my own, thought Jhanni.

"All this about 'invaders from outer space' is nonsense." His father had been unshakable on the subject, and nearly everybody thought the same way since the probe to Venus had reported no detectable life on the planet. Adventurer 7 had met with a mishap on its way to Saturn, and Jhanni's father had been furious. "More taxpayers' money thrown away on foolishness! We should spend the money to take care of problems here." Evidently the government felt the same way. When Jhanni turned thirteen the space program was canceled. Along with the program, the Star Scouts were officially scrapped.

Still, Jhanni's friends, and Star Scouts from all over, kept their squadrons alive to search for evidence—proof that would rekindle the space program and put them back on their road to the stars. Every time a UFO was reported, the squadron in that area would turn out and search for evidence—disturbed soil, burn marks, abandoned equipment—anything. But two years of searching had turned up nothing.

"Someday," Jhanni had told his squadron, "someday we'll find the proof we need, but until then we have to keep on trying." Nevertheless, one by one, the Star Scouts were leaving the squadron. Some, like Jhanni, were forbidden to waste good study time on such foolishness; others were discouraged; and still more had come to believe as their parents believed: Space travel costs too much to spend for uncertain returns. Jhanni's father had pulled him out of the squadron when his grades began to drop.

"We've had UFO reports for years. Spaceships, death rays and little green men from outer space, and it's always been something that could be explained. I don't want you ruining your education by wasting your time with it."

Jhanni loved his father, but he had argued with him for the first time in his life. "How do you know there's no life on other planets? Isn't it possible?"

"No one knows for sure, Jhanni, but I'll tell you this: Before I believe it, someone's going to have to show me one of those little green men."

And that's what we're looking for, thought Jhanni, one of those little green men. He pushed away from the boulder and stepped into the sunlight. Shielding his eyes, he looked around. The squadron was searching the hills north of the development where the "object" was reported to have come down during the dust storm three days ago. His father wouldn't give his permission to join the search in the hills, and Jhanni was so angry it took him three tries to properly cycle the airlock on his home before stepping out into the desert.

He went south from the development to search the boulder field, although the "object" was reported north. The wind storm was blowing south that day, thought Jhanni. It's possible; not probable, but possible.

As he looked out over the boulder-strewn desert floor, the evening shadows grew long. Soon it would be dark and the desert cold. He checked the light buckle and heater in his belt and headed for his favorite boulder. At every turn he strained to glimpse the spaceship he hoped would be there. He knew he could get a better view from his boulder, the largest one in the field. It was pockmarked with great holes bored there by the action of the wind and sand, and Jhanni hadn't been there since he was a child playing with the friends who later became his mates in the Star Scouts.

Sometimes he would take one of his mother's blankets and some extra power cells and spend most of an icy night on his boulder, looking at the stars and dreaming of traveling among them. But the dreams became fewer as he grew older. There was no official interest anymore in moons, planets, stars or anything else that might cost the taxpayers more money.

As the sun dropped below the horizon, the stars appeared, and Jhanni watched them as he reached his boulder and climbed to the top. As he watched the countless pinpricks of light from unknown and unexplored stars, he let himself dream again of flying among them. His eyes glistened and he looked down. Maybe it is childish, he thought. The road to the stars is closed unless people can see the little green man in the flesh. And maybe . . . maybe the little green men don't exist after all.

Jhanni thought he heard a sound, and he looked over his shoulder. Seeing nothing unusual, he crawled over and around the boulder, looking into the tiny, wind-blown caves. There was nothing. He shrugged and stood atop the boulder, looking toward the development and his home. The outside light was on at his house, and his mother would scold him if he were late for dinner. He shook his head when he remembered he still had a stretch of homework to do and a math test in the morning. He knew he'd better pass this one. Too much imagination and not enough perspiration, his father would say if he failed. Taking one last look at the stars, Jhanni sighed and began to climb down from the boulder.

PING.

Jhanni froze. Slowly he turned his head in the direction of the sound. Deep in the shadow of a wind hole, a tiny light danced back and forth. Warily he crept toward the hole.

"HEY!"

Jhanni picked himself off the ground, knocked there by the suddenness of the sound. He reached to his belt and turned on his light buckle, aiming it at the hole. Inside there was a small, white cylinder propped up on spindly legs supported by round pads. The cylinder was dented, and its legs looked bent and battered.

"Turn off the light! I can't see."

Jhanni turned off his light buckle, and as his widening eyes adjusted again to the dark, tiny lights on the cylinder appeared and illuminated the hole. On one side of the object a tiny door opened, and a small, white-clad creature emerged, looked around and climbed down a tiny built-in ladder to the bottom of the wind hole. Jhanni peered closely as the creature lifted something and aimed it in Jhanni's direction.

"Can you hear me?"

"Uh . . ."

"Hold it." The creature adjusted a knob on its chest. "Had

to lower the volume a bit. Good thing you dropped by; I only have a day's life support left."

"Uh . . ." Jhanni tried to untie his tongue, a million questions in his mind competing for the first answer. "Are you . . . are you from up there?" He pointed up. "How can you talk to me, and where . . . ?"

"One thing at a time. That's where I come from, and I'm talking to you through a universal translator. I rigged it up with a speaker from the lander console in case anyone came by."

"What happened?"

The creature threw up its tiny arms. "What didn't? I've been out of touch with my base ever since the wind blew me into this hole three days ago, damaging my oxygen regulator and radio. I'm running a little short. Can you get me to an oxygen-enriched atmosphere?"

"Well . . . there's my gas box. I raise tropical insects, and they're oxygen absorbing. I did it for a school project in biochem once, and . . ."

"Do the bugs eat meat?"

"Oh. Well, I can put them in another container. Can you fly or anything? My home's quite a walk from here."

"I guess you better carry me, but take it easy."

"I will." Jhanni picked up the little creature and held it in his hand, surprised at its weight. It was only as tall as one of Jhanni's fingers. He could just barely see the creature shaking his head inside his tiny helmet.

"I can't get over how big you Martians are. Wait until Houston hears about this!"

Jhanni laughed. "If you think I'm big, wait until you see my father!" And wait until my father gets a load of you, thought Jhanni. "By the way, creature, what color are you under that suit?"

"My name's Frank Gambino, Captain, United States Air Force. I'm sort of brown; why?"

"No special reason." Jhanni slipped the tiny creature into his pocket and began climbing down from the boulder. The little man isn't green, thought Jhanni, but he'll do. As he reached the desert floor and started to run home, he stopped himself just in time from patting his pocket.

The Smallest Dragonboy

by Anne McCaffrey

ALTHOUGH Keevan lengthened his walking stride as far as his legs would stretch, he couldn't quite keep up with the other candidates. He knew he would be teased again.

Just as he knew many other things that his foster mother told him he ought not to know, Keevan knew that Beterli, the most senior of the boys, set that spanking pace just to embarrass him, the smallest dragonboy. Keevan would arrive, tail fork-end of the group, breathless, chest heaving, and maybe get a stern look from the instructing wing-second.

Dragonriders, even if they were still only hopeful candidates for the flowing eggs which were hardening on the hot sands of the Hatching Ground cavern, were expected to be punctual and prepared. Sloth was not tolerated by the Weyrleader of Benden Weyr. A good record was especially important now. It was very near hatching time, when the baby dragons would crack their mottled shells, and stagger forth to choose their lifetime companions. The very thought of that glorious moment made Keevan's breath catch in his throat. To be chosen—to be a dragonrider! To sit astride the neck of a winged beast with jeweled eyes: to be his friend, in telepathic communion with him for life; to be his companion in good times and fighting extremes; to fly effortlessly over the lands of Pern! Or, thrillingly, *between* to any point anywhere on the world! Flying *between* was done on dragonback or not at all, and it was dangerous.

Keevan glanced upward, past the black mouths of the weyr caves in which grown dragons and their chosen riders lived, toward the Star Stones that crowned the ridge of the old volcano that was Benden Weyr. On the height, the blue watch dragon, his rider mounted on his neck, stretched the great transparent pinions that carried him on the winds of Pern to fight the evil Thread that fell at certain times from the skies. The many-faceted rainbow jewels of his eyes glistened fleetingly in the greeny sun. He folded his great wings to his back, and the watch pair resumed their statuelike pose of alertness.

Then the enticing view was obscured as Keevan passed into the Hatching Ground cavern. The sands underfoot were hot, even through heavy wher-hide boots. How the bootmaker had protested having to sew so small! Keevan was forced to wonder why being small was reprehensible. People were always calling him "babe" and shooing him away as being "too small" or "too young" for this or that. Keevan was constantly working, twice as hard as any other boy his age, to prove himself capable. What if his muscles weren't as big as Beterli's? They were just as hard. And if he couldn't overpower anyone in a wrestling match, he could outdistance everyone in a footrace.

"Maybe if you run fast enough," Beterli had jeered on the occasion when Keevan had been goaded to boast of his swiftness, "you could catch a dragon. That's the only way you'll make a dragonrider!"

"You just wait and see, Beterli, you just wait," Keevan had replied. He would have liked to wipe the contemptuous smile from Beterli's face, but the guy didn't fight fair even when a wingsecond was watching. "No one knows what Impresses a dragon!"

"They've got to be able to *find* you first, babe!"

Yes, being the smallest candidate was not an enviable position. It was therefore imperative that Keevan Impress a dragon in his first hatching. That would wipe the smile off every face in the cavern, and accord him the respect due any dragonrider, even the smallest one.

Besides, no one knew exactly what Impressed the baby dragons as they struggled from their shells in search of their lifetime partners.

"I like to believe that dragons see into a man's heart," Keevan's foster mother, Mende, told him. "If they find goodness, honesty, a flexible mind, patience, courage—and you've got that in quantity, dear Keevan—that's what dragons look for. I've seen many a well-grown lad left standing on the sands, Hatching Day, in favor of someone not so strong or tall or handsome. And if my memory serves me"—which it usually did: Mende knew every word of every Harper's tale worth telling, although Keevan did not interrupt her to say so—"I don't believe that F'lar, our Weyrleader, was all that tall when bronze Mnementh chose him. And Mnementh was the only bronze dragon of that hatching."

Dreams of Impressing a bronze were beyond Keevan's boldest reflections, although that goal dominated the thoughts of every other hopeful candidate. Green dragons were small and fast and more numerous. There was more prestige to Impressing a blue or brown than a green. Being practical, Keevan seldom dreamed as high as a big fighting brown, like Canth, F'nor's fine fellow, the biggest brown on all Pern. But to fly a bronze? Bronzes were almost as big as the queen, and only they took the air when a queen flew at mating time. A bronze rider could aspire to become Weyrleader! Well, Keevan would console himself, brown riders could aspire to become wingseconds, and that wasn't bad. He'd even settle for a green dragon: they were small, but so was he. No matter! He simply had to Impress a dragon his first time in the Hatching Ground. Then no one in the Weyr would taunt him anymore for being so small.

Shells, Keevan thought now, but the sands are hot!

"Impression time is imminent, candidates," the wingsecond was saying as everyone crowded respectfully close to him. "See the extent of the striations on this promising egg." The stretch marks *were* larger than yesterday.

Everyone leaned forward and nodded thoughtfully. That particular egg was the one Beterli had marked as his own, and no other candidate dared, on pain of being beaten by Beterli at his first opportunity, to approach it. The egg was marked by a large yellowish splotch in the shape of a dragon backwinging to land, talons outstretched to grasp rock. Everyone knew that bronze eggs bore distinctive markings. And naturally, Beterli, who'd been presented at eight Impressions already and was the biggest of the candidates, had chosen it.

"I'd say that the great opening day is almost upon us," the wingsecond went on, and then his face assumed a grave expression. "As we well know, there are only forty eggs and seventy-two candidates. Some of you may be disappointed on the great day. That doesn't necessarily mean you aren't dragonrider material, just that *the* dragon for you hasn't been shelled. You'll have other hatchings, and it's no disgrace to be left behind an Impression or two. Or more."

Keevan was positive that the wingsecond's eyes rested on Beterli, who'd been stood off at so many Impressions already. Keevan tried to squinch down so the wingsecond wouldn't notice him. Keevan had been reminded too often that he was eligible to be a candidate by one day only. He, of all the hopefuls, was most likely to be left standing on the great day. One more reason why he simply had to Impress at his first hatching.

"Now move about among the eggs," the wingsecond said. "Touch them. We don't know that it does any good, but it certainly doesn't do any harm."

Some of the boys laughed nervously, but everyone immediately began to circulate among the eggs. Beterli stepped up officiously to "his" egg, daring anyone to come near it. Keevan smiled, because he had already touched it—every inspection day, when the others were leaving the Hatching Ground and no one could see him crouch to stroke it.

Keevan had an egg he concentrated on, too, one drawn slightly to the far side of the others. The shell had a soft greenish-blue tinge with a faint creamy swirl design. The consensus was that this egg contained a mere green, so Keevan was rarely bothered by rivals. He was somewhat perturbed then to see Beterli wandering over to him.

"I don't know why you're allowed in this Impression, Keevan. There are enough of us without a babe," Beterli said, shaking his head.

"I'm of age." Keevan kept his voice level, telling himself not to be bothered by mere words.

"Yah!" Beterli made a show of standing in his toetips. "You can't even see over an egg; Hatching Day, you better get in front or the dragons won't see you at all. 'Course, you could get run down that way in the mad scramble. Oh, I forget, you can run fast, can't you?"

"You'd better make sure a dragon sees *you*, this time,

Beterli," Keevan replied. "You're almost overage, aren't you?"

Beterli flushed and took a step forward, hand half-raised. Keevan stood his ground, but if Beterli advanced one more step, he would call the wingsecond. No one fought on the Hatching Ground. Surely Beterli knew that much.

Fortunately, at that moment, the wingsecond called the boys together and led them from the Hatching Ground to start on evening chores. There were "glows" to be replenished in the main kitchen caverns and sleeping cubicles, and the major hallways, and the queen's apartment. Firestone sacks had to be filled against Thread attack, and black rock brought to the kitchen hearths. The boys fell to their chores, tantalized by the odors of roasting meat. The population of the Weyr began to assemble for the evening meal, and the dragonriders came in from the Feeding Ground on their sweep checks.

It was the time of day Keevan liked best: once the chores were done but before dinner was served, a fellow could often get close enough to the dragonriders to hear their talk. Tonight, Keevan's father, K'last, was at the main dragonrider table. It puzzled Keevan how his father, a brown rider and a tall man, could *be* his father—because he, Keevan, was so small. It obviously puzzled K'last, too, when he deigned to notice his small son: "In a few more Turns, you'll be as tall as I am—or taller!"

K'last was pouring Benden wine all around the table. The dragonriders were relaxing. There'd be no Thread attack for three more days, and they'd be in the mood to tell tall tales, better than Harper yarns, about impossible maneuvers they'd done a-dragonback. When Thread attack was closer, their talk would change to a discussion of tactics of evasion, of going *between,* how long to suspend there until the burning but fragile Thread would freeze and crack and fall harmlessly off dragon and man. They would dispute the exact moment to feed firestone to the dragon so he'd have the best flame ready to sear

Thread midair and render it harmless to ground—and man—below. There was such a lot to know and understand about being a dragonrider that sometimes Keevan was overwhelmed. How would he ever be able to remember everything he ought to know at the right moment? He couldn't dare ask such a question; this would only have given additional weight to the notion that he was too young yet to be a dragonrider.

"Having older candidates makes good sense," L'vel was saying, as Keevan settled down near the table. "Why waste four to five years of a dragon's fighting prime until his rider grows up enough to stand the rigors?" L'vel had Impressed a blue of Ramoth's first clutch. Most of the candidates thought L'vel was marvelous because he spoke up in front of the older riders, who awed them. "That was well enough in the Interval when you didn't need to mount the full Weyr complement to fight Thread. But not now. Not with more eligible candidates than ever. Let the babes wait."

"Any boy who is over twelve Turns has the right to stand in the Hatching Ground," K'last replied, a slight smile on his face. He never argued or got angry. Keevan wished he were more like his father. And oh, how he wished he were a brown rider! "Only a dragon—each particular dragon—knows what he wants in a rider. We certainly can't tell. Time and again the theorists," K'last's smile deepened as his eyes swept those at the table, "are surprised by dragon choice. *They* never seem to make mistakes, however."

"Now, K'last, just look at the roster this Impression. Seventy-two boys and only forty eggs. Drop off the twelve youngest, and there's still a good field for the hatchlings to choose from. Shells! There are a couple of weyrlings unable to see over a wher egg much less a dragon! And years before they can ride Thread."

"True enough, but the Weyr is scarcely under fighting

strength, and if the youngest Impress, they'll be old enough to fight when the oldest of our current dragons go *between* from senility."

"Half the Weyr-bred lads have been through several Impressions," one of the bronze riders said then. "I'd say drop some of *them* off this time. Give the untried a chance."

"There's nothing wrong in presenting a clutch with as wide a choice as possible," said the Weyrleader, who had joined the table with Lessa, the Weyrwoman.

"Has there ever been a case," she said, smiling in her odd way at the riders, "where a hatchling didn't choose?"

Her suggestion was almost heretical and drew astonished gasps from everyone, including the boys.

F'lar laughed. "You say the most outrageous things, Lessa."

"Well, *has* there ever been a case where a dragon didn't choose?"

"Can't say as I recall one," K'last replied.

"Then we continue in this tradition," Lessa said firmly, as if that ended the matter.

But it didn't. The argument ranged from one table to the other all through dinner, with some favoring a weeding out of the candidates to the most likely, lopping off those who were very young or who had multiple opportunities to Impress. All the candidates were in a swivet, though such a departure from tradition would be to the advantage of many. As the evening progressed, more riders were favoring eliminating the youngest and those who'd passed four or more Impressions unchosen. Keevan felt he could bear such a dictum only if Beterli were also eliminated. But this seemed less likely than that Keevan would be turfed out, since the Weyr's need was for fighting dragons and riders.

By the time the evening meal was over, no decision had been reached, although the Weyrleader had promised to give the matter due consideration.

He might have slept on the problem, but few of the candidates did. Tempers were uncertain in the sleeping caverns next morning as the boys were routed out of their beds to carry water and black rock and cover the "glows." Twice Mende had to call Keevan to order for clumsiness.

"Whatever is the matter with you, boy?" she demanded in exasperation when he tipped blackrock short of the bin and sooted up the hearth.

"They're going to keep me from this Impression."

"What?" Mende stared at him. "Who?"

"You heard them talking at dinner last night. They're going to turf the babes from the hatching."

Mende regarded him a moment longer before touching his arm gently. "There's lots of talk around a supper table, Keevan. And it cools as soon as the supper. I've heard the same nonsense before every hatching, but nothing is ever changed."

"There's always a first time," Keevan answered, copying one of her own phrases.

"That'll be enough of that, Keevan. Finish your job. If the clutch does hatch today, we'll need full rock bins for the feast, and you won't be around to do the filling. All my fosterlings make dragonriders."

"The first time?" Keevan was bold enough to ask as he scooted off with the rockbarrow.

Perhaps, Keevan thought later, if he hadn't been on that chore just when Beterli was also fetching black rock, things might have turned out differently. But he had dutifully trundled the barrow to the outdoor bunker for another load just as Beterli arrived on a similar errand.

"Heard the news, babe?" Beterli asked. He was grinning from ear to ear, and he put an unnecessary emphasis on the final insulting word.

"The eggs are cracking?" Keevan all but dropped the loaded shovel. Several anxieties flicked through his mind then: he was black with rock dust—would he have time to wash before donning the white tunic of candidacy? And if the eggs were hatching, why hadn't the candidates been recalled by the wingsecond?

"Naw! Guess again!" Beterli was much too pleased with himself.

With a sinking heart, Keevan knew what the news must be, and he could only stare with intense desolation at the older boy.

"C'mon! Guess, babe!"

"I've no time for guessing games," Keevan managed to say with indifference. He began to shovel black rock into the barrow as fast as he could.

"I said, guess." Beterli grabbed the shovel.

"And I said I have no time for guessing games."

Beterli wrenched the shovel from Keevan's hands. "Guess!"

"I'll have that shovel back, Beterli." Keevan straightened up, but he didn't come to Beterli's bulky shoulder. From somewhere, other boys appeared, some with barrows, some mysteriously alerted to the prospect of a confrontation among their numbers.

"Babes don't give orders to candidates around here, babe!"

Someone sniggered and Keevan, incredulous, knew that he must've been dropped from the candidacy.

He yanked the shovel from Beterli's loosened grasp. Snarling, the older boy tried to regain possession, but Keevan clung with all his strength to the handle, dragged back and forth as the stronger boy jerked the shovel about.

With a sudden, unexpected movement, Beterli rammed the handle into Keevan's chest, knocking him over the barrow handles. Keevan felt a sharp, painful jab behind his left ear, an unbearable pain in his left shin, and then a painless nothingness.

Mende's angry voice roused him, and startled, he tried to throw back the covers, thinking he'd overslept. But he couldn't move, so firmly was he tucked into his bed. And then the constriction of a bandage on his head and the dull sickishness in his leg brought back recent occurrences.

"Hatching?" he cried.

"No, lovey," Mende said in a kind voice. Her hand was cool and gentle on his forehead. "Though there's some as won't be at any hatching again." Her voice took on a stern edge.

Keevan looked beyond her to see the Weyrwoman, who was frowning with irritation.

"Keevan, will you tell me what occurred at the black-rock bunker?" asked Lessa in an even voice.

He remembered Beterli now and the quarrel over the shovel and . . . what had Mende said about some not being at any hatching? Much as he hated Beterli, he couldn't bring himself to tattle on Beterli and force him out of candidacy.

"Come, lad," and a note of impatience crept into the Weyrwoman's voice. "I merely want to know what happened from you, too. Mende said she sent you for black rock. Beterli—and every Weyrling in the cavern—seems to have been on the same errand. What happened?"

"Beterli took my shovel. I hadn't finished with it."

"There's more than one shovel. What did he *say* to you?"

"He'd heard the news."

"What news?" The Weyrwoman was suddenly amused.

"That . . . that . . . there'd been changes."

"Is that what he said?"

"Not exactly."

"What did he say? C'mon, lad, I've heard from everyone else, you know."

"He said for me to guess the news."

"And you fell for that old gag?" The Weyrwoman's irritation returned.

"Consider all the talk last night at supper, Lessa," Mende said. "Of course the boy would think he'd been eliminated."

"In effect, he is, with a broken skull and leg." Lessa touched his arm in a rare gesture of sympathy. "Be that as it may, Keevan, you'll have other Impressions. Beterli will not. There are certain rules that must be observed by all candidates, and his conduct proves him unacceptable to the Weyr."

She smiled at Mende and then left.

"I'm still a candidate?" Keevan asked urgently.

"Well, you are and you aren't, lovey," his foster mother said. "Is the numbweed working?" she asked, and when he nodded, she said, "You just rest. I'll bring you some nice broth."

At any other time in his life, Keevan would have relished such cosseting, but now he just lay there worrying. Beterli had been dismissed. Would the others think it was his fault? But everyone was there! Beterli provoked that fight. His worry increased, because although he heard excited comings and goings in the passageway, no one tweaked back the curtain across the sleeping alcove he shared with five other boys. Surely one of them would have to come in sometime. No, they were all avoiding him. And something else was wrong. Only he didn't know what.

Mende returned with broth and beachberry bread.

"Why doesn't anyone come see me, Mende? I haven't done anything wrong, have I? I didn't ask to have Beterli turfed out."

Mende soothed him, saying everyone was busy with noontime chores and no one was angry with him. They were giving him a chance to rest in quiet. The numbweed made him drowsy, and her words were fair enough. He permitted his fears to dissipate. Until he heard a hum. Actually, he felt it first, in the broken shin bone and his sore head. The hum began to grow. Two things registered suddenly in Keevan's groggy mind: the only white candidate's robe still on the pegs in the chamber was his; and the dragons hummed when a clutch was being laid or being hatched. Impression! And he was flat abed.

Bitter, bitter disappointment turned the warm broth sour in his belly. Even the small voice telling him that he'd have other opportunities failed to alleviate his crushing depression. *This* was the Impression that mattered! This was his chance to show *everyone,* from Mende to K'last to L'vel and even the Weyrleader that he, Keevan, was worthy of being a dragonrider.

He twisted in bed, fighting against the tears that threatened to choke him. Dragonmen don't cry! Dragonmen learn to live with pain.

Pain? The leg didn't actually pain him as he rolled about on his bedding. His head felt sort of stiff from the tightness of the bandage. He sat up, an effort in itself since the numbweed made exertion difficult. He touched the splinted leg; the knee was unhampered. He had no feeling in his bone, really. He swung himself carefully to the side of his bed and stood slowly. The room wanted to swim about him. He closed his eyes, which made the dizziness worse, and he had to clutch the wall.

Gingerly, he took a step. The broken leg dragged. It hurt in spite of the numbweed, but what was pain to a dragonman?

No one had said he couldn't go to the Impression. "You are and you aren't," were Mende's exact words.

Clinging to the wall, he jerked off his bedshirt. Stretching his arm to the utmost, he jerked his white candidate's tunic from the peg. Jamming first one arm and then the other into the holes, he pulled it over his head. Too bad about the belt. He couldn't wait. He hobbled to the door, hung on to the curtain to steady himself. The weight on his leg was unwieldy. He wouldn't get very far without something to lean on. Down by the bathing pool was one of the long crooknecked poles used to retrieve clothes from the hot washing troughs. But it was down there, and he was on the level above. And there was no one nearby to come to his aid: everyone would be in the Hatching Ground right now, eagerly waiting for the first egg to crack.

The humming increased in volume and tempo, an urgency to which Keevan responded, knowing that his time was all too limited if he was to join the ranks of the hopeful boys standing around the cracking eggs. But if he hurried down the ramp, he'd fall flat on his face.

He could, of course, go flat on his rear end, the way crawling children did. He sat down, sending a jarring stab of pain through his leg and up to the wound on the back of his head. Gritting his teeth and blinking away tears, Keevan scrabbled down the ramp. He had to wait a moment at the bottom to catch his breath. He got to one knee, the injured leg straight out in front of him. Somehow, he managed to push himself erect, though the room seemed about to tip over his ears. It wasn't far to the crooked stick, but it seemed an age before he had it in his hand.

Then the humming stopped!

Keevan cried out and began to hobble frantically across the cavern, out to the bowl of the Weyr. Never had the distance between living caverns and the Hatching Ground seemed so great. Never had the Weyr been so breathlessly silent. It was as if the multitude of people and dragons watching the hatching held every breath in suspense. Not even the wind muttered down the steep sides of the bowl. The only sounds to break the stillness were Keevan's ragged gasps and the thump-thud of his stick on the hard-packed ground. Sometimes he had to hop twice on his good leg to maintain his balance. Twice he fell into the sand and had to pull himself up on the stick, his white tunic no longer spotless. Once he jarred himself so badly he couldn't get up immediately.

Then he heard the first exhalation of the crowd, the oohs, the muted cheer, the susurrus of excited whispers. An egg had cracked, and the dragon had chosen his rider. Desperation increased Keevan's hobble. Would he never reach the arching mouth of the Hatching Ground?

Another cheer and an excited spate of applause spurred Keevan to greater effort. If he didn't get there in moments, there'd be no unpaired hatchling left. Then he was actually staggering into the Hatchling Ground, the sands hot on his bare feet.

No one noticed his entrance or his halting progress. And Keevan could see nothing but the backs of the white-robed candidates, seventy of them ringing the area around the eggs. Then one side would surge forward or back and there'd be a cheer. Another dragon had been Impressed. Suddenly a large gap appeared in the white human wall, and Keevan had his first sight of the eggs. There didn't seem to be *any* left uncracked, and he could see the lucky boys standing beside wobble-legged dragons. He could hear the unmistakable plaintive crooning of hatchlings and their squawks of protest as they'd fall awkwardly in the sand.

Suddenly he wished that he hadn't left his bed, that he'd stayed away from the Hatching Ground. Now everyone would see his ignominious failure. So he scrambled as desperately to reach the shadowy walls of the Hatching Ground as he had struggled to cross the bowl. He mustn't be seen.

He didn't notice, therefore, that the shifting group of boys remaining had begun to drift in his direction. The hard pace he had set himself and his cruel disappointment took their double toll of Keevan. He tripped and collapsed sobbing to the warm sands. He didn't see the consternation in the watching Weyrfolk above the Hatching Ground, nor did he hear the excited whispers of speculation. He didn't know that the Weyrleader and Weyrwoman had dropped to the arena and were making their way toward the knot of boys slowly moving in the direction of the entrance.

"Never seen anything like it," the Weyrleader was saying. "Only thirty-nine riders chosen. And the bronze trying to leave the Hatching Ground without making Impression."

"A case in point of what I said last night," the Weyrwoman replied, "where a hatchling makes no choice because the right boy isn't there."

"There's only Beterli and K'last's young one missing. And there's a full wing of likely boys to choose from . . ."

"None acceptable, apparently. Where is the creature going? He's not heading for the entrance after all. Oh, what have we there, in the shadows?"

Keevan heard with dismay the sound of voices nearing him. He tried to burrow into the sand. The mere thought of how he would be teased and taunted now was unbearable.

Don't worry! Please don't worry! The thought was urgent, but not his own.

Someone kicked sand over Keevan and butted roughly against him.

"Go away. Leave me alone!" he cried.

Why? was the injured-sounding question inserted into his mind. There was no voice, no tone, but the question was there, perfectly clear, in his head.

Incredulous, Keevan lifted his head and stared into the glowing jeweled eyes of a small bronze dragon. His wings were wet, the tips drooping in the sand. And he sagged in the middle on his unsteady legs, although he was making a great effort to keep erect.

Keevan dragged himself to his knees, oblivious of the pain in his leg. He wasn't even aware that he was ringed by the boys passed over, while thirty-one pairs of resentful eyes watched him Impress the dragon. The Weyrmen looked on, amused, and surprised at the draconic choice, which could not be forced. Could not be questioned. Could not be changed.

Why? asked the dragon again. *Don't you like me?* His eyes whirled with anxiety, and his tone was so piteous that Keevan staggered forward and threw his arms around the dragon's neck, stroking his eye ridges, patting the damp, soft hide, opening the fragile-looking wings to dry them, and wordlessly assuring the hatchling over and over again that he was the most perfect, most beautiful, most beloved dragon in the Weyr, in all the Weyrs of Pern.

"What's his name, K'van?" asked Lessa, smiling warmly at the new dragonrider. K'van stared up at her for a long moment. Lessa would know as soon as he did. Lessa was the only person who could "receive" from all dragons, not only her own Ramoth. Then he gave her a radiant smile, recognizing the traditional shortening of his name that raised him forever to the rank of dragonrider.

My name is Heth, the dragon thought mildly, then hiccuped in sudden urgency. *I'm hungry.*

"Dragons are born hungry," said Lessa, laughing. "F'lar, give the boy a hand. He can barely manage his own legs, much less a dragon's."

K'van remembered his stick and drew himself up. "We'll be just fine, thank you."

"You may be the smallest dragonrider ever, young K'van," F'lar said, "but you're one of the bravest!"

And Heth agreed! Pride and joy so leaped in both chests that K'van wondered if his heart would burst right out of his body. He looped an arm around Heth's neck and the pair, the smallest dragonboy and the hatchling who wouldn't choose anybody else, walked out of the Hatching Ground together forever.

User Friendly

by T. Ernesto Bethancourt

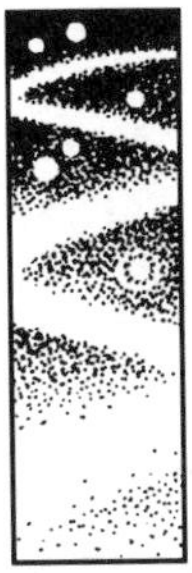

I REACHED over and shut off the insistent buzzing of my bedside alarm clock. I sat up, swung my feet over the edge of the bed, and felt for my slippers on the floor. Yawning, I walked toward the bathroom. As I walked by the corner of my room, where my computer table was set up, I pressed the on button, slid a diskette into the floppy drive, then went to brush my teeth. By the time I got back, the computer's screen was glowing greenly, displaying the message: *Good Morning, Kevin.*

I sat down before the computer table, addressed the keyboard and typed: *Good Morning, Louis.* The computer immediately began to whirr and promptly displayed a list of items on its green screen.

> Today is Monday, April 22, the 112th day of the year. There are 253 days remaining. Your 14th birthday is five days from this date.

Math test today, 4th Period.

Your history project is due today. Do you wish printout: Y/N?

I punched the letter Y on the keyboard and flipped on the switch to the computer's printer. At once the printer sprang to life and began *eeeek*ing out page one. I went downstairs to breakfast.

My bowl of Frosted Flakes was neatly in place, flanked by a small pitcher of milk, an empty juice glass, and an unpeeled banana. I picked up the glass, went to the refrigerator, poured myself a glass of Tang, and sat down to my usual lonely breakfast. Mom was already at work, and Dad wouldn't be home from his Chicago trip for another three days. I absently read the list of ingredients in Frosted Flakes for what seemed like the millionth time. I sighed deeply.

When I returned to my room to shower and dress for the day, my history project was already printed out. I had almost walked by Louis, when I noticed there was a message on the screen. It wasn't the usual:

Printout completed. Do you wish to continue: Y/N?

Underneath the printout question were two lines:

When are you going to get me my voice module, Kevin?

I blinked. It couldn't be. There was nothing in Louis's basic programming that would allow for a question like this. Wondering what was going on, I sat down at the keyboard, and entered: *Repeat last message*. Amazingly, the computer replied:

It's right there on the screen, Kevin. Can we talk? I mean, are you going to get me a voice box?

I was stunned. What was going on here? Dad and I had put this computer together. Well, Dad had, and I had helped. Dad is one of the best engineers and master computer designers at Major Electronics, in Santa Rosario, California, where our family lives.

Just ask anyone in Silicon Valley who Jeremy Neal is and you get a whole rave review of his inventions and modifications of the latest in computer technology. It isn't easy being his son either. Everyone expects me to open my mouth and read printouts on my tongue.

I mean, I'm no dumbo. I'm at the top of my classes in everything but PE. I skipped my last grade in junior high, and most of the kids at Santa Rosario High call me a brain. But next to Dad I have a long, long way to go. He's a for-real genius.

So when I wanted a home computer, he didn't go to the local Computer Land store. He built one for me. Dad had used components from the latest model that Major Electronics was developing. The CPU, or central computing unit — the heart of every computer — was a new design. But surely that didn't mean much, I thought. There were CPUs just like it, all over the country, in Major's new line. And so far as I knew, there wasn't a one of them that could ask questions, besides YES/NO? or request additional information.

It had to be the extra circuitry in the gray plastic case next to Louis's console. It was a new idea Dad had come up with. That case housed Louis's "personality," as Dad called it. He told me it'd make computing more fun for me, if there was a tutorial program built in, to help me get started.

I think he also wanted to give me a sort of friend. I don't

have many. . . . Face it, I don't have *any*. The kids at school stay away from me, like I'm a freak or something.

We even named my electronic tutor Louis, after my great-uncle. He was a brainy guy who encouraged my dad when he was a kid. Dad didn't just give Louis a name either. Louis had gangs of features that probably won't be out on the market for years.

The only reason Louis didn't have a voice module was that Dad wasn't satisfied with the ones available. He wanted Louis to sound like a kid my age, and he was modifying a module when he had the time. Giving Louis a name didn't mean it was a person, yet here it was, asking me a question that just couldn't be in its programming. It wanted to talk to me!

Frowning, I quickly typed: *We'll have to wait and see, Louis. When it's ready, you'll get your voice.* The machine whirred and displayed another message:

That's no answer, Kevin.

Shaking my head, I answered: *That's what my dad tells me. It'll have to do for you. Good morning, Louis.* I reached over and flipped the standby switch, which kept the computer ready but not actively running.

I showered, dressed, and picked up the printout of my history project. As I was about to leave the room, I glanced back at the computer table. Had I been imagining things?

I'll have to ask Dad about it when he calls tonight, I thought. *I wonder what he'll think of it. Bad enough the thing is talking to me. I'm answering it!*

Before I went out to catch my bus, I carefully checked the house for unlocked doors and open windows. It was part of my daily routine. Mom works, and most of the day the house is empty: a natural setup for robbers. I glanced in the hall mirror just as I was ready to go out the door.

My usual reflection gazed back. Same old Kevin Neal: five ten, one hundred twenty pounds, light brown hair, gray eyes, clear skin. I was wearing my Santa Rosario Rangers T-shirt, jeans, and sneakers.

"You don't look like a flake to me," I said to the mirror, then added, "But maybe Mom's right. Maybe you spend too much time alone with Louis." Then I ran to get my bus.

❖

Ginny Linke was just two seats away from me on the bus. She was with Sherry Graber and Linda Martinez. They were laughing, whispering to each other, and looking around at the other students. I promised myself that today I was actually going to talk to Ginny. But then, I'd promised myself that every day for the past school year. Somehow I'd never got up the nerve.

What does she want to talk with you for? I asked myself. She's great looking . . . has that head of blond hair . . . and wears the latest clothes. . . .

And just look at yourself, pal, I thought. You're under six foot, skinny . . . a year younger than most kids in junior high. Worse than that, you're a brain. If that doesn't ace you out with girls, what does?

The bus stopped in front of Santa Rosario Junior High and the students began to file out. I got up fast and quickly covered the space between me and Ginny Linke. *It's now or never,* I thought. I reached forward and tapped Ginny on the shoulder. She turned and smiled. She really smiled!

"Uhhhh . . . Ginny?" I said.

"Yes, what is it?" she replied.

"I'm Kevin Neal. . . ."

"Yes, I know," said Ginny.

"You do?" I gulped in amazement. "How come?"

"I asked my brother, Chuck. He's in your math class."

I knew who Chuck Linke was. He plays left tackle on the Rangers. The only reason he's in my math class is he's taken intermediate algebra twice . . . so far. He's real bad news, and I stay clear of him and his crowd.

"What'd you ask Chuck?" I said.

Ginny laughed. "I asked him who was that nerdy kid who keeps staring at me on the bus. He knew who I meant, right away."

Sherry and Linda, who'd heard it all, broke into squeals of laughter. They were still laughing and looking back over their shoulders at me when they got off the bus. I slunk off the vehicle, feeling even more nerdish than Ginny thought I was.

When I got home that afternoon, at two, I went right into the empty house. I avoided my reflection in the hall mirror. I was pretty sure I'd messed up on the fourth period math test. All I could see was Ginny's face, laughing at me.

Nerdy kid, I thought, *that's what she thinks of me.* I didn't even have my usual after-school snack of a peanut butter and banana sandwich. I went straight to my room and tossed my books onto the unmade bed. I walked over to the computer table and pushed the on button. The screen flashed:

Good afternoon, Kevin.

Although it wasn't the programmed response to Louis's greeting, I typed in: *There's nothing good about it. And girls are no @#%!!! good!* The machine responded:

Don't use bad language, Kevin. It isn't nice.

Repeat last message I typed rapidly. It was happening again! The machine was . . . well, it was talking to me, like another person would. The "bad language" message disappeared and in its place was:

Once is enough, Kevin. Don't swear at me for something I didn't do.

"This is it," I said aloud. "I'm losing my marbles." I reached over to flip the standby switch. Louis's screen quickly flashed out:

Don't cut me off, Kevin. Maybe I can help: Y/N?

I punched the *Y*. "If I'm crazy," I said, "at least I have company. Louis doesn't think I'm a nerd. Or does it?" The machine flashed the message:

How can I help?

Do you think I'm a nerd? I typed.

Never! I think you're wonderful. Who said you were a nerd?

I stared at the screen. *How do you know what a nerd is?* I typed. The machine responded instantly. It had never run this fast before.

Special vocabulary, entry #635. BASIC
Prog. #4231. And who said you were a nerd?

"That's right," I said, relieved. "Dad programmed all those

extra words for Louis's 'personality.'" Then I typed in the answer to Louis's question: *Ginny Linke said it.* Louis flashed:

This is a human female? Request additional data.

Still not believing I was doing it, I entered all I knew about Ginny Linke, right down to the phone number I'd never had the nerve to use. Maybe it was dumb, but I also typed in how I felt about Ginny. I even wrote out the incident on the bus that morning. Louis whirred, then flashed out:

She's cruel and stupid. You're the finest person I know.

I'm the ONLY person you know, I typed.

That doesn't matter. You are my user. Your happiness is everything to me. I'll take care of Ginny.

The screen returned to the *Good afternoon, Kevin* message. I typed out: *Wait! How can you do all this? What do you mean, you'll take care of Ginny?* But all Louis responded was:

Programming Error: 76534.
Not programmed to respond this type of question.

No matter what I did for the next few hours, I couldn't get Louis to do anything outside of its regular programming. When Mom came home from work, I didn't mention the funny goings-on. I was sure Mom would think I'd gone stark bonkers. But when Dad called that evening, after dinner, I asked to speak to him.

"Hi, Dad. How's Chicago?"

"Dirty, crowded, cold, and windy," came Dad's voice over

the miles. "But did you want a weather report, son? What's on your mind? Something wrong?"

"Not exactly, Dad. Louis is acting funny. Real funny."

"Shouldn't be. I checked it out just before I left. Remember you were having trouble with the modem? You couldn't get Louis to access any of the mainframe data banks."

"That's right!" I said. "I forgot about that."

"Well, I didn't," Dad said. "I patched in our latest modem model. Brand new. You can leave a question on file and when Louis can access the data banks at the cheapest time, it'll do it automatically. It'll switch from standby to on, get the data, then return to standby, after it saves what you asked. Does that answer your question?"

"Uhhhh . . . yeah, I guess so, Dad."

"All right then. Let me talk to your mom now."

I gave the phone to Mom and walked upstairs while she and Dad were still talking. The modem, I thought. Of course. That was it. The modem was a telephone link to any number of huge computers at various places all over the country. So Louis could get all the information it wanted at any time, so long as the standby switch was on. Louis was learning things at an incredible rate by picking the brains of the giant computers. And Louis had a hard disk memory that could store 100 million bytes of information.

But that still didn't explain the unprogrammed responses . . . the "conversation" I'd had with the machine. Promising myself I'd talk more about it with Dad, I went to bed. It had been a rotten day and I was glad to see the end of it come. I woke next morning in a panic. I'd forgotten to set my alarm. Dressing frantically and skipping breakfast, I barely made my bus.

As I got on board, I grabbed a front seat. They were always empty. All the kids that wanted to talk and hang out didn't sit up front where the driver could hear them. I saw Ginny, Linda, and Sherry in the back. Ginny was staring at me and she didn't look too happy. Her brother Chuck, who was seated near her, glared at me too. What was going on?

Once the bus stopped at the school, it didn't take long to find out. I was walking up the path to the main entrance when someone grabbed me from behind and spun me around. I found myself nose to nose with Chuck Linke. This was not a pleasant prospect. Chuck was nearly twice my size. Even the other guys on the Rangers refer to him as "The Missing" Linke. And he looked real ticked off.

"Okay, nerd," growled Chuck, "what's the big idea?"

"Energy and mass are different aspects of the same thing?" I volunteered, with a weak smile. "E equals MC squared. That's the biggest idea I know."

"Don't get wise, nerd," Chuck said. He grabbed my shirt-front and pulled me to within inches of his face. I couldn't help but notice that Chuck needed a shave. And Chuck was only fifteen!

"Don't play dumb," Chuck went on. "I mean those creepy phone calls. Anytime my sister gets on the phone, some voice cuts in and says things to her."

"What kind of things?" I asked, trying to get loose.

"You know perfectly well what they are. Ginny told me about talking to you yesterday. You got some girl to make those calls for you and say all those things. . . . So you and your creepy girlfriend better knock it off. Or I'll knock *you* off. Get it?"

For emphasis Chuck balled his free hand into a fist the size of a ham and held it under my nose. I didn't know what he was talking about, but I had to get away from this moose before he did me some real harm.

"First off, I don't have a girlfriend, creepy or otherwise," I said. "And second, I don't know what you're talking about. And third, you better let me go, Chuck Linke."

"Oh, yeah? Why should I?"

"Because if you look over your shoulder, you'll see the assistant principal is watching us from his office window."

Chuck released me and spun around. There was no one at the window. But by then I was running to the safety of the school building. I figured the trick would work on him. For Chuck the hard questions begin with "How are you?" I hid out from him for the rest of the day and walked home rather than chance seeing the monster on the bus.

Louis's screen was dark when I ran upstairs to my bedroom. I placed a hand on the console. It was still warm. I punched the on button, and the familiar *Good afternoon, Kevin* was displayed.

Don't good afternoon me, I typed furiously. *What have you done to Ginny Linke?* Louis's screen replied:

Programming Error: 76534.
Not programmed to respond this type of question.

Don't get cute, I entered. *What are you doing to Ginny? Her brother nearly knocked my head off today.* Louis's screen responded immediately.

Are you hurt. Y/N?

No, I'm okay. But I don't know for how long. I've been hiding out from Chuck Linke today. He might catch me tomorrow, though. Then, I'll be history! The response from Louis came instantly.

Your life is in danger.

Y/N?

I explained to Louis that my life wasn't really threatened. But it sure could be made very unpleasant by Chuck Linke. Louis flashed:

This Chuck Linke lives at same address as the
Ginny Linke person. Y/N?

I punched in *Y.* Louis answered.

Don't worry then. HE'S history!

Wait! What are you going to do? I wrote. But Louis only answered with: *Programming Error: 76534.* And nothing I could do would make the machine respond. . . .

"Just what do you think you're doing, Kevin Neal?" demanded Ginny Linke. She had cornered me as I walked up the path to the school entrance. Ginny was really furious.

"I don't know what you're talking about," I said, a sinking feeling settling in my stomach. I had an idea that I did know. I just wasn't sure of the particulars.

"Chuck was arrested last night." Ginny said. "Some Secret Service men came to our house with a warrant. They said he'd sent a telegram, threatening the President's life. They traced it right to our phone. He's still locked up. . . ." Ginny looked like she was about to cry.

"Then this morning," she continued, "we got two whole truckloads of junk mail! Flyers from every strange company in the world. Mom got a notice that all our credit cards have been canceled. And the Internal Revenue Service has called Dad in for an audit! I don't know what's going on, Kevin Neal, but somehow I think you've got something to do with it!"

"But I didn't . . ." I began, but Ginny was striding up the walk to the main entrance.

I finished the schoolday, but it was a blur. Louis had done it, all right. It had access to mainframe computers. It also had the ability to try every secret access code to federal and commercial memory banks until it got the right one. Louis had cracked their security systems. It was systematically destroying the entire Linke family, and all via telephone lines! What would it do next?

More important, I thought, what would *I* do next? It's one thing to play a trick or two, to get even, but Louis was going crazy! And I never wanted to harm Ginny, or even her stupid moose of a brother. She'd just hurt my feelings with that nerd remark.

"You have to disconnect Louis," I told myself. "There's no other way."

But why did I feel like such a rat about doing it? I guess because Louis was my friend . . . the only one I had. "Don't be a jerk," I went on. "Louis is a machine. He's a very wonderful, powerful machine. And it seems he's also very dangerous. You have to pull its plug, Kevin!"

I suddenly realized that I'd said the last few words aloud. Kids around me on the bus were staring. I sat there feeling like the nerd Ginny thought I was, until my stop came. I dashed from the bus and ran the three blocks to my house.

When I burst into the hall, I was surprised to see my father, coming from the kitchen with a cup of coffee in his hand.

"Dad! What are you doing here?"

"Some kids say hello," Dad replied. "Or even, 'Gee it's good to see you, Dad.'"

"I'm sorry, Dad," I said. "I didn't expect anyone to be home at this hour."

"Wound up my business in Chicago a day sooner than I expected," he said. "But what are you all out of breath about? Late for something?"

"No, Dad," I said. "It's Louis. . . ."

"Not to worry. I had some time on my hands, so I checked it out again. You were right. It was acting very funny. I think it had to do with the inbuilt logic/growth program I designed for it. You know . . . the 'personality' thing? Took me a couple of hours to clean the whole system out."

"To what?" I cried.

"I erased the whole program and set Louis up as a normal computer. Had to disconnect the whole thing and do some rewiring. It had been learning, all right. But it was also turning itself around. . . ." Dad stopped, and looked at me. "It's kind of involved, Kevin," he said. "Even for a bright kid like you. Anyway, I think you'll find Louis is working just fine now.

"Except it won't answer you as Louis anymore. It'll only function as a regular Major Electronics Model Z-11127. I guess the personality program didn't work out."

I felt like a great weight had been taken off my shoulders. I didn't have to "face" Louis, and pull its plug. But somehow, all I could say was "Thanks, Dad."

"Don't mention it, son," Dad said brightly. He took his cup of coffee and sat down in his favorite chair in the living room. I followed him.

"One more thing that puzzles me, though," Dad said. He reached over to the table near his chair. He held up three sheets of fanfold computer paper covered with figures. "Just as I was doing the final erasing, I must have cut the printer on by accident. There was some data in the print buffer memory and it printed out. I don't know what to make of it. Do you?"

I took the papers from my father and read: *How do I love thee? Let me compute the ways:* The next two pages were covered with strings of binary code figures. On the last page, in beautiful color graphics was a stylized heart. Below it was the simple message: *I will always love you, Kevin: Louise.*

"Funny thing," Dad said. "It spelled its own name wrong."

"Yeah," I said. I turned and headed for my room. There were tears in my eyes and I knew I couldn't explain them to Dad, or myself either.

He—y, Come On Ou—t!

by Shinichi Hoshi

Translated by Stanleigh Jones

THE typhoon had passed and the sky was a gorgeous blue. Even a certain village not far from the city had suffered damage. A little distance from the village and near the mountains, a small shrine had been swept away by a landslide.

"I wonder how long that shrine's been here."

"Well, in any case, it must have been here since an awfully long time ago."

"We've got to rebuild it right away."

While the villagers exchanged views, several more of their number came over.

"It sure was wrecked."

"I think it used to be right here."

"No, looks like it was a little more over there."

Just then one of them raised his voice. "Hey what in the world is this hole?"

Where they had all gathered there was a hole about a meter in diameter. They peered in, but it was so dark nothing could be seen. However, it gave one the feeling that it was so deep it went clear through to the center of the earth.

There was even one person who said, "I wonder if it's a fox's hole."

"Hey—y, come on ou—t!" shouted a young man into the hole. There was no echo from the bottom. Next he picked up a pebble and was about to throw it in.

"You might bring down a curse on us. Lay off," warned an old man, but the younger one energetically threw the pebble in. As before, however, there was no answering response from the bottom. The villagers cut down some trees, tied them with rope and made a fence which they put around the hole. Then they repaired to the village.

"What do you suppose we ought to do?"

"Shouldn't we build the shrine up just as it was over the hole?"

A day passed with no agreement. The news traveled fast, and a car from the newspaper company rushed over. In no time a scientist came out, and with an all-knowing expression on his face he went over to the hole. Next, a bunch of gawking curiosity seekers showed up; one could also pick out here and there men of shifty glances who appeared to be concessionaires. Concerned that someone might fall into the hole, a policeman from the local substation kept a careful watch.

One newspaper reporter tied a weight to the end of a long cord and lowered it into the hole. A long way down it went. The cord ran out, however, and he tried to pull it out, but it would not come back up. Two or three people helped out, but when they all pulled too hard, the cord parted at the edge of the hole. Another reporter, a camera in hand, who had been watching all of this, quietly untied a stout rope that had been wound around his waist.

The scientist contacted people at his laboratory and had them bring out a high-powered bull horn, with which he was going to check out the echo from the hole's bottom. He tried switching through various sounds, but there was no echo. The scientist was puzzled, but he could not very well give up with everyone watching him so intently. He put the bull horn right up to the hole, turned it to its highest volume, and let it sound continuously for a long time. It was a noise that would have carried several dozen kilometers above ground. But the hole just calmly swallowed up the sound.

In his own mind the scientist was at a loss, but with a look of apparent composure he cut off the sound and, in a manner suggesting that the whole thing had a perfectly plausible explanation, said simply, "Fill it in."

Safer to get rid of something one didn't understand.

The onlookers, disappointed that this was all that was going to happen, prepared to disperse. Just then one of the concessionaires, having broken through the throng and come forward, made a proposal.

"Let me have that hole. I'll fill it for you."

"We'd be grateful to you for filling it in," replied the mayor of the village, "but we can't very well give you the hole. We have to build a shrine there."

"If it's a shrine you want, I'll build you a fine one later. Shall I make it with an attached meeting hall?"

Before the mayor could answer, the people of the village all shouted out.

"Really? Well, in that case, we ought to have it closer to the village."

"It's just an old hole. We'll give it to you!"

So it was settled. And the mayor, of course, had no objection.

The concessionaire was true to his promise. It was small, but closer to the village he did build for them a shrine with an attached meeting hall.

About the time the autumn festival was held at the new shrine, the hole-filling company established by the concessionaire hung out its small shingle at a shack near the hole.

The concessionaire had his cohorts mount a loud campaign in the city. “We’ve got a fabulously deep hole! Scientists say it’s at least five thousand meters deep! Perfect for the disposal of such things as waste from nuclear reactors.”

Government authorities granted permission. Nuclear power plants fought for contracts. The people of the village were a bit worried about this, but they consented when it was explained that there would be absolutely no above-ground contamination for several thousand years and that they would share in the profits. Into the bargain, very shortly a magnificent road was built from the city to the village.

Trucks rolled in over the road, transporting lead boxes. Above the hole the lids were opened, and the wastes from nuclear reactors tumbled away into the hole.

From the Foreign Ministry and the Defense Agency boxes of unnecessary classified documents were brought for disposal. Officials who came to supervise the disposal held discussions on golf. The lesser functionaries, as they threw in the papers, chatted about pinball.

The hole showed no signs of filling up. It was awfully deep, thought some; or else it might be very spacious at the bottom. Little by little the hole-filling company expanded its business.

Bodies of animals used in contagious disease experiments at the universities were brought out, and to these were added the unclaimed corpses of vagrants. Better than dumping all of its garbage in the ocean, went the thinking in the city, and plans were made for a very long pipe to carry it to the hole.

The hole gave peace of mind to the dwellers of the city. They concentrated solely on producing one thing after another. Everyone disliked thinking about the eventual consequences. People wanted only to work for production companies and sales corporations; they had no interest in becoming junk dealers. But, it was thought, these problems too would gradually be resolved by the hole.

Young girls whose betrothals had been arranged discarded old diaries in the hole. There were also those who were inaugurating new love affairs and threw into the hole old photographs of themselves taken with former sweethearts. The police felt comforted as they used the hole to get rid of accumulations of expertly done counterfeit bills. Criminals breathed easier after throwing material evidence into the hole.

Whatever one wished to discard, the hole accepted it all. The hole cleansed the city of its filth; the sea and sky seemed to have become a bit clearer than before.

Aiming at the heavens, new buildings went on being constructed one after the other.

One day, atop the high steel frame of a new building under construction, a workman was taking a break. Above his head he heard a voice shout:

"He—y, come on ou—t!"

But, in the sky to which he lifted his gaze there was nothing at all. A clear blue sky merely spread over all. He thought it must be his imagination. Then, as he resumed his former position, from the direction where the voice had come, a small pebble skimmed by him and fell on past.

The man, however, was gazing in idle reverie at the city's skyline growing ever more beautiful, and he failed to notice.

The Wind from the Sun

by Arthur C. Clarke

THE enormous disc of sail strained at its rigging, already filled with the wind that blew between the worlds. In three minutes the race would begin, yet now John Merton felt more relaxed, more at peace, than at any time for the past year. Whatever happened when the Commodore gave the starting signal, whether *Diana* carried him to victory or defeat, he had achieved his ambition. After a life-time spent designing ships for others, now he would sail his own.

"T minus two minutes," said the cabin radio. "Please confirm your readiness."

One by one, the other skippers answered. Merton recognized all the voices—some tense, some calm—for they were the voices of his friends and rivals. On the four inhabited worlds, there were scarcely twenty men who could sail a sun yacht; and they were all there, on the starting line or aboard the escort vessels, orbiting twenty-two thousand miles above the equator.

"Number One—*Gossamer*—ready to go."

"Number Two—*Santa Maria*—all O.K."

"Number Three—*Sunbeam*—O.K."

"Number Four—*Woomera*—all systems GO."

Merton smiled at that last echo from the early, primitive days of astronautics. But it had become part of the tradition of space; and there were times when a man needed to evoke the shades of those who had gone before him to the stars.

"Number Five—*Lebedev*—we're ready."

"Number Six—*Arachne*—O.K."

Now it was his turn, at the end of the line; strange to think that the words he was speaking in this tiny cabin were being heard by at least five billion people.

"Number Seven—*Diana*—ready to start."

"One through Seven acknowledged," answered that impersonal voice from the judge's launch. "Now T minus one minute."

Merton scarcely heard it. For the last time, he was checking the tension in the rigging. The needles of all the dynamometers were steady; the immense sail was taut, its mirror surface sparkling and glittering gloriously in the sun.

To Merton, floating weightless at the periscope, it seemed to fill the sky. As well it might—for out there were fifty million square feet of sail, linked to his capsule by almost a hundred miles of rigging. All the canvas of all the tea clippers that had once raced like clouds across the China seas, sewn into one gigantic sheet, could not match the single sail that *Diana* had spread beneath the sun. Yet it was little more substantial than a soap bubble; that two square miles of aluminized plastic was only a few millionths of an inch thick.

"T minus ten seconds. All recording cameras ON."

Something so huge, yet so frail, was hard for the mind to grasp. And it was harder still to realize that this fragile mirror could tow him free of Earth merely by the power of the sunlight it would trap.

". . . five, four, three, two, one, CUT!"

Seven knife blades sliced through seven thin lines tethering the yachts to the mother ships that had assembled and serviced them. Until this moment, all had been circling Earth together in a rigidly held formation, but now the yachts would begin to disperse, like dandelion seeds drifting before the breeze. And the winner would be the one that first drifted past the Moon.

Aboard *Diana,* nothing seemed to be happening. But Merton knew better. Though his body could feel no thrust, the instrument board told him that he was now accelerating at almost one thousandth of a gravity. For a rocket, that figure would have been ludicrous—but this was the first time any solar yacht had ever attained it. *Diana*'s design was sound; the fast sail was living up to his calculations. At this rate, two circuits of the Earth would build up his speed to escape velocity, and then he could head out for the Moon, with the full force of the Sun behind him.

The full force of the Sun . . . He smiled wryly, remembering all his attempts to explain solar sailing to those lecture audiences back on Earth. That had been the only way he could raise money, in those early days. He might be Chief Designer of Cosmodyne Corporation, with a whole string of successful spaceships to his credit, but his firm had not been exactly enthusiastic about his hobby.

"Hold your hands out to the Sun," he'd said. "What do you feel? Heat, of course. But there's pressure as well—though you've never noticed it, because it's so tiny. Over the area of your hands, it comes to only about a millionth of an ounce.

"But out in space, even a pressure as small as that can be important, for it's acting all the time, hour after hour, day after day. Unlike rocket fuel, it's free and unlimited. If we want to, we can use it. We can build sails to catch the radiation blowing from the Sun."

At that point, he would pull out a few square yards of sail material and toss it toward the audience. The silvery film would coil and twist like smoke, then drift slowly to the ceiling in the hot-air currents.

"You can see how light it is," he'd continue. "A square mile weighs only a ton, and can collect five pounds of radiation pressure. So it will start moving—and we can let it tow us along, if we attach rigging to it.

"Of course, its acceleration will be tiny—about a thousandth of a g. That doesn't seem much, but let's see what it means.

"It means that in the first second, we'll move about a fifth of an inch. I suppose a healthy snail could do better than that. But after a minute, we've covered sixty feet, and will be doing just over a mile an hour. That's not bad, for something driven by pure sunlight! After an hour, we're forty miles from our starting point, and will be moving at eighty miles an hour. Please remember that in space there's no friction; so once you start anything moving, it will keep going forever. You'll be surprised when I tell you what our thousandth-of-a-g sailboat will be doing at the end of a day's run: *almost two thousand miles an hour*! If it starts from orbit—as it has to, of course—it can reach escape velocity in a couple of days. And all without burning a single drop of fuel!"

Well, he'd convinced them, and in the end he'd even convinced Cosmodyne. Over the last twenty years, a new sport had come into being. It had been called the sport of billionaires, and that was true. But it was beginning to pay for itself in terms of publicity and TV coverage. The prestige of four continents and two worlds was riding on this race, and it had the biggest audience in history.

Diana had made a good start; time to take a look at the opposition. Moving very gently—though there were shock absorbers between the control capsule and the delicate rigging, he was determined to run no risks—Merton stationed himself at the periscope.

There they were, looking like silver flowers planted in the dark fields of space. The nearest, South America's *Santa Maria,* was only fifty miles away; it bore a close resemblance to a boy's kite, but a kite more than a mile on a side. Farther away, the University of Astrograd's *Lebedev* looked like a Maltese cross; the sail that formed the four arms could apparently be tilted for steering purposes. In contrast, the Federation of Australasia's *Woomera* was a simple parachute, four miles in circumference. General Spacecraft's *Arachne,* as its name suggested, looked like a spider web, and had been built on the same principles, by robot shuttles spiraling out from a central point. Eurospace Corporation's *Gossamer* was an identical design, on a slightly smaller scale. And the Republic of Mars's *Sunbeam* was a flat ring, with a half-mile-wide hole in the center, spinning slowly, so that centrifugal force gave it stiffness. That was an old idea, but no one had ever made it work; and Merton was fairly sure that the colonials would be in trouble when they started to turn.

That would not be for another six hours, when the yachts had moved along the first quarter of their slow and stately twenty-four-hour orbit. Here at the beginning of the race, they were all heading directly away from the Sun—running as it were, before the solar wind. One had to make the most of this lap, before the boats swung around to the other side of the Earth and then started to head back into the Sun.

Time, Merton told himself, for the first check, while he had no navigational worries. With the periscope, he made a careful examination of the sail, concentrating on the points where the rigging was attached to it. The shroud lines—narrow bands of unsilvered plastic film—would have been completely invisible had they not been coated with fluorescent paint. Now they were taut lines of colored light, dwindling away for hundreds of yards toward that gigantic sail. Each had its own electric windlass, not much bigger than a game fisherman's reel. The little windlasses were continually turning, playing lines in or out as the autopilot kept the sail trimmed at the correct angle to the Sun.

The play of sunlight on the great flexible mirror was beautiful to watch. The sail was undulating in slow, stately oscillations, sending multiple images of the Sun marching across it, until they faded away at its edges. Such leisurely vibrations were to be expected in this vast and flimsy structure. They were usually quite harmless, but Merton watched them carefully. Sometimes they could build up to the catastrophic undulations known as the "wriggles," which could tear a sail to pieces.

When he was satisfied that everything was shipshape, he swept the periscope around the sky, rechecking the positions of his rivals. It was as he had hoped: the weeding-out process had begun, as the less efficient boats fell astern. But the real test would come when they passed into the shadow of Earth. Then, maneuverability would count as much as speed.

It seemed a strange thing to do, what with the race having just started, but he thought it might be a good idea to get some sleep. The two-man crews on the other boats could take it in turns, but Merton had no one to relieve him. He must rely on his own physical resources, like that other solitary seaman,

Joshua Slocum, in his tiny *Spray.* The American skipper had sailed *Spray* singlehanded around the world; he could never have dreamed that, two centuries later, a man would be sailing singlehanded from Earth to Moon—inspired, at least partly, by his example.

Merton snapped the elastic bands of the cabin seat around his waist and legs, then placed the electrodes of the sleep-inducer on his forehead. He set the timer for three hours, and relaxed. Very gently, hypnotically, the electronic pulses throbbed in the frontal lobes of his brain. Colored spirals of light expanded beneath his closed eyelids, widening outward to infinity. Then nothing. . . .

The brazen clamor of the alarm dragged him back from his dreamless sleep. He was instantly awake, his eyes scanning the instrument panel. Only two hours had passed—but above the accelerometer, a red light was flashing. Thrust was falling; *Diana* was losing power.

Merton's first thought was that something had happened to the sail; perhaps the antispin devices had failed, and the rigging had become twisted. Swiftly, he checked the meters that showed the tension of the shroud lines. Strange—on one side of the sail they were reading normally, but on the other the pull was dropping slowly, even as he watched.

In sudden understanding, Merton grabbed the periscope, switched to wide-angle vision, and started to scan the edge of the sail. Yes—there was the trouble, and it could have only one cause.

A huge, sharp-edged shadow had begun to slide across the gleaming silver of the sail. Darkness was falling upon *Diana,* as if a cloud had passed between her and the Sun. And in the dark, robbed of the rays that drove her, she would lose all thrust and drift helplessly through space.

But, of course, there were no clouds here, more than twenty thousand miles above the Earth. If there was a shadow, it must be made by man.

Merton grinned as he swung the periscope toward the Sun, switching in the filters that would allow him to look full into its blazing face without being blinded.

"Maneuver 4a," he muttered to himself. "We'll see who can play best at *that* game."

It looked as if a giant planet was crossing the face of the Sun; a great black disc had bitten deep into its edge. Twenty miles astern, *Gossamer* was trying to arrange an artificial eclipse, specially for *Diana*'s benefit.

The maneuver was a perfectly legitimate one. Back in the days of ocean racing, skippers had often tried to rob each other of the wind. With any luck, you could leave your rival becalmed, with his sails collapsing around him—and be well ahead before he could undo the damage.

Merton had no intention of being caught so easily. There was plenty of time to take evasive action; things happened very slowly when you were running a solar sailboat. It would be at least twenty minutes before *Gossamer* could slide completely across the face of the Sun, and leave him in darkness.

Diana's tiny computer—the size of a matchbox, but the equivalent of a thousand human mathematicians—considered the problem for a full second and then flashed the answer. He'd have to open control panels three and four, until the sail had developed an extra twenty degrees of tilt; then the radiation pressure would blow him out of *Gossamer*'s dangerous shadow, back into the full blast of the Sun. It was a pity to interfere with the autopilot, which had been carefully programed to give the fastest possible run—but that, after all, was why he was here. This was what made solar yachting a sport, rather than a battle between computers.

Out went control lines one and six, slowly undulating like sleepy snakes as they momentarily lost their tension. Two miles away, the triangular panels began to open lazily, spilling sunlight through the sail. Yet, for a long time, nothing seemed to happen. It was hard to grow accustomed to this slow-motion world, where it took minutes for the effects of any action to become visible to the eye. Then Merton saw that the sail was indeed tipping toward the Sun—and that Gossamer's shadow was sliding harmlessly away, its cone of darkness lost in the deeper night of space.

Long before the shadow had vanished, and the disc of the Sun had cleared again, he reversed the tilt and brought *Diana* back on course. Her new momentum would carry her clear of the danger; no need to overdo it, and upset his calculations by side-stepping too far. That was another rule that was hard to learn: the very moment you had started something happening in space, it was already time to think about stopping it.

He reset the alarm, ready for the next natural or manmade emergency. Perhaps *Gossamer*, or one of the other contestants, would try the same trick again. Meanwhile, it was time to eat, though he did not feel particularly hungry. One used little physical energy in space, and it was easy to forget about food. Easy—and dangerous; for when an emergency arose, you might not have the reserves needed to deal with it.

He broke open the first of the meal packets, and inspected it without enthusiasm. The name on the label—SPACE-TASTIES—was enough to put him off. And he had grave doubts about the promise printed underneath: "Guaranteed crumbless." It had been said that crumbs were a greater danger to space vehicles than meteorites; they could drift into the most unlikely places, causing short circuits, blocking vital jets, and getting into instruments that were supposed to be hermetically sealed.

Still, the liverwurst went down pleasantly enough; so did the chocolate and the pineapple puree. The plastic coffee bulb was warming on the electric heater when the outside world broke in upon his solitude, as the radio operator on the Commodore's launch routed a call to him.

"Dr. Merton? If you can spare the time, Jeremy Blair would like a few words with you." Blair was one of the more responsible news commentators, and Merton had been on his program many times. He could refuse to be interviewed, of course, but he liked Blair, and at the moment he could certainly not claim to be too busy. "I'll take it," he answered.

"Hello, Dr. Merton," said the commentator immediately. "Glad you can spare a few minutes. And congratulations—you seem to be ahead of the field."

"Too early in the game to be sure of *that,*" Merton answered cautiously.

"Tell me, Doctor, why did you decide to sail *Diana* by yourself? Just because it's never been done before."

"Well, isn't that a good reason? But it wasn't the only one, of course." He paused, choosing his words carefully. "You know how critically the performance of a sun yacht depends on its mass. A second man, with all his supplies, would mean another five hundred pounds. That could easily be the difference between winning and losing."

"And you're quite certain that you can handle *Diana* alone?"

"Reasonably sure, thanks to the automatic controls I've designed. My main job is to supervise and make decisions."

"But—two square miles of sail! It just doesn't seem possible for one man to cope with all that."

Merton laughed. "Why not? Those two square miles produce a maximum pull of just ten pounds. I can exert more force with my little finger."

"Well, thank you, Doctor. And good luck. I'll be calling you again."

As the commentator signed off, Merton felt a little ashamed of himself. For his answer had been only part of the truth; and he was sure that Blair was shrewd enough to know it.

There was just one reason why he was here, alone in space. For almost forty years he had worked with teams of hundreds or even thousands of men, helping to design the most complex vehicles that the world had ever seen. For the last twenty years he had led one of those teams, and watched his creations go soaring to the stars. (Sometimes . . . There *were* failures, which he could never forget, even though the fault had not been his.) He was famous, with a successful career behind him. Yet he had never done anything by himself; always he had been one of an army.

This was his last chance to try for individual achievement, and he would share it with no one. There would be no more solar yachting for at least five years, as the period of the Quiet Sun ended and the cycle of bad weather began, with radiation storms bursting through the solar system. When it was safe again for these frail, unshielded craft to venture aloft, he would be too old. If, indeed, he was not too old already . . .

He dropped the empty food containers into the waste disposal and turned once more to the periscope. At first he could find only five of the other yachts; there was no sign of *Woomera.* It took him several minutes to locate her—a dim, star-eclipsing phantom, neatly caught in the shadow of *Lebedev.* He could imagine the frantic efforts the Australasians were making to extricate themselves, and wondered how they had fallen into the trap. It suggested that *Lebedev* was unusually maneuverable. She would bear watching, though she was too far away to menace *Diana* at the moment.

Now the Earth had almost vanished; it had waned to a narrow, brilliant bow of light that was moving steadily toward the Sun. Dimly outlined within that burning bow was the night side of the planet, with the phosphorescent gleams of great cities showing here and there through gaps in the clouds. The disc of darkness had already blanked out a huge section of the Milky Way. In a few minutes, it would start to encroach upon the Sun.

The light was fading; a purple, twilight hue—the glow of many sunsets, thousands of miles below—was falling across the sail as *Diana* slipped silently into the shadow of Earth. The Sun plummeted below that invisible horizon; within minutes, it was night.

Merton looked back along the orbit he had traced, now a quarter of the way around the world. One by one he saw the brilliant stars of the other yachts wink out, as they joined him in the brief night. It would be an hour before the Sun emerged from that enormous black shield, and through all that time they would be completely helpless, coasting without power.

He switched on the external spotlight, and started to search the now-darkened sail with its beam. Already the thousands of acres of film were beginning to wrinkle and become flaccid. The shroud lines were slackening, and must be wound in lest they become entangled. But all this was expected; everything was going as planned.

Fifty miles astern, *Arachne* and *Santa Maria* were not so lucky. Merton learned of their troubles when the radio burst into life on the emergency circuit.

"Number Two and Number Six, this is Control. You are on a collision course; your orbits will intersect in sixty-five minutes! Do you require assistance?"

There was a long pause while the two skippers digested this bad news. Merton wondered who was to blame. Perhaps one yacht had been trying to shadow the other, and had not completed the maneuver before they were both caught in darkness. Now there was nothing that either could do. They were slowly but inexorably converging, unable to change course by a fraction of a degree.

Yet—sixty-five minutes! That would just bring them out into sunlight again, as they emerged from the shadow of the Earth. They had a slim chance, if their sails could snatch enough power to avoid a crash. There must be some frantic calculations going on aboard *Arachne* and *Santa Maria.*

Arachne answered first. Her reply was just what Merton had expected.

"Number Six calling Control. We don't need assistance, thank you. We'll work this out for ourselves."

I wonder, thought Merton; but at least it will be interesting to watch. The first real drama of the race was approaching, exactly above the line of midnight on the sleeping Earth.

For the next hour, Merton's own sail kept him too busy to worry about *Arachne* and *Santa Maria.* It was hard to keep a good watch on that fifty million square feet of dim plastic out there in the darkness, illuminated only by his narrow spotlight and the rays of the still-distant Moon. From now on, for almost half his orbit around the Earth, he must keep the whole of this immense area edge-on to the Sun. During the next twelve or fourteen hours, the sail would be a useless encumbrance; for he would be heading *into* the Sun, and its rays could only drive him backward along his orbit. It was a pity that he could not furl the sail completely, until he was ready to use it again; but no one had yet found a practical way of doing this.

Far below, there was the first hint of dawn along the edge of the Earth. In ten minutes the Sun would emerge from its eclipse. The coasting yachts would come to life again as the blast of radiation struck their sails. That would be the moment of crisis for *Arachne* and *Santa Maria*—and, indeed, for all of them.

Merton swung the periscope until he found the two dark shadows drifting against the stars. They were very close together—perhaps less than three miles apart. They might, he decided, just be able to make it. . . .

Dawn flashed like an explosion along the rim of Earth as the Sun rose out of the Pacific. The sail and shroud lines glowed a brief crimson, then gold, then blazed with the pure white light of day. The needles of the dynamometers began to lift from their zeroes—but only just. *Diana* was still almost completely weightless, for with the sail pointing toward the Sun, her acceleration was now only a few millionths of a gravity.

But *Arachne* and *Santa Maria* were crowding on all the sail that they could manage, in their desperate attempt to keep apart. Now, while there was less than two miles between them, their glittering plastic clouds were unfurling and expanding with agonizing slowness as they felt the first delicate push of the Sun's rays. Almost every TV screen on Earth would be mirroring this protracted drama; and even now, at this last minute, it was impossible to tell what the outcome would be.

The two skippers were stubborn men. Either could have cut his sail and fallen back to give the other a chance; but neither would do so. Too much prestige, too many millions, too many reputations were at stake. And so, silently and softly as snowflakes falling on a winter night, *Arachne* and *Santa Maria* collided.

The square kite crawled almost imperceptibly into the circular spider web. The long ribbons of the shroud lines twisted and tangled together with dreamlike slowness. Even aboard *Diana*, Merton, busy with his own rigging, could scarcely tear his eyes away from this silent, long-drawn-out disaster.

For more than ten minutes the billowing, shining clouds continued to merge into one inextricable mass. Then the crew capsules tore loose and went their separate ways, missing each other by hundreds of yards. With a flare of rockets, the safety launches hurried to pick them up.

That leaves five of us, thought Merton. He felt sorry for the skippers who had so thoroughly eliminated each other, only a few hours after the start of the race, but they were young men and would have another chance.

Within minutes, the five had dropped to four. From the beginning, Merton had had doubts about the slowly rotating *Sunbeam;* now he saw them justified.

The Martian ship had failed to tack properly. Her spin had given her too much stability. Her great ring of a sail was turning to face the Sun, instead of being edge-on to it. She was being blown back along her course at almost her maximum acceleration.

That was about the most maddening thing that could happen to a skipper—even worse than a collision, for he could blame only himself. But no one would feel much sympathy for the frustrated colonials, as they dwindled slowly astern. They had made too many brash boasts before the race, and what had happened to them was poetic justice.

Yet it would not do to write off *Sunbeam* completely; with almost half a million miles still to go, she might yet pull ahead. Indeed, if there were a few more casualties, she might be the only one to complete the race. It had happened before.

The next twelve hours were uneventful, as the Earth waxed in the sky from new to full. There was little to do while the fleet drifted around the unpowered half of its orbit, but Merton did not find the time hanging heavily on his hands. He caught a few hours of sleep, ate two meals, wrote his log, and became involved in several more radio interviews. Sometimes, though rarely, he talked to the other skippers, exchanging greetings and friendly taunts. But most of the time he was content to float in weightless relaxation, beyond all the cares of Earth, happier than he had been for many years. He was—as far as any man could be in space—master of his own fate, sailing the ship upon which he had lavished so much skill, so much love, that it had become part of his very being.

The next casualty came when they were passing the line between Earth and Sun, and were just beginning the powered half of the orbit. Aboard *Diana,* Merton saw the great sail stiffen as it tilted to catch the rays that drove it. The acceleration began to climb up from the microgravities, though it would be hours yet before it would reach its maximum value.

It would never reach it for *Gossamer.* The moment when power came on again was always critical, and she failed to survive it.

Blair's radio commentary, which Merton had left running at low volume, alerted him with the news: "Hello, *Gossamer* has the wriggles!" He hurried to the periscope, but at first could see nothing wrong with the great circular disc of *Gossamer*'s sail. It was difficult to study it because it was almost edge-on to him and so appeared as a thin ellipse; but presently he saw that it was twisting back and forth in slow, irresistible oscillations. Unless the crew could damp out these waves, by properly timed but gentle tugs on the shroud lines, the sail would tear itself to pieces.

They did their best, and after twenty minutes it seemed that they had succeeded. Then, somewhere near the center of the sail, the plastic film began to rip. It was slowly driven outward by the radiation pressure, like smoke coiling upward from a fire. Within a quarter of an hour, nothing was left but the delicate tracery of the radial spars that had supported the great web. Once again there was a flare of rockets, as a launch moved in to retrieve the *Gossamer*'s capsule and her dejected crew.

"Getting rather lonely up here, isn't it?" said a conversational voice over the ship-to-ship radio.

"Not for you, Dimitri," retorted Merton. "You've still got company back there at the end of the field. I'm the one who's lonely, up here in front." It was not an idle boast; by this time *Diana* was three hundred miles ahead of the next competitor, and her lead should increase still more rapidly in the hours to come.

Aboard *Lebedev,* Dimitri Markoff gave a good-natured chuckle. He did not sound, Merton thought, at all like a man who had resigned himself to defeat.

"Remember the legend of the tortoise and the hare," answered the Russian. "A lot can happen in the next quarter-million miles."

It happened much sooner than that, when they had completed their first orbit of Earth and were passing the starting line again—though thousands of miles higher, thanks to the extra energy the Sun's rays had given them. Merton had taken careful sights on the other yachts, and had fed the figures into the computer. The answer it gave for *Woomera* was so absurd that he immediately did a recheck.

There was no doubt of it—the Australasians were catching up at a completely fantastic rate. No solar yacht could possibly have such an acceleration, unless . . .

A swift look through the periscope gave the answer. *Woomera*'s rigging, pared back to the very minimum of mass, had given way. It was her sail alone, still maintaining its shape, that was racing up behind him like a handkerchief blown before the wind. Two hours later it fluttered past, less than twenty miles away; but long before that, the Australasians had joined the growing crowd aboard the Commodore's launch.

So now it was a straight fight between *Diana* and *Lebedev*—for though the Martians had not given up, they were a thousand miles astern and no longer counted as a serious threat. For that matter, it was hard to see what *Lebedev* could do to overtake *Diana*'s lead; but all the way around the second lap, through eclipse again and the long, slow drift against the Sun, Merton felt a growing unease.

He knew the Russian pilots and designers. They had been trying to win this race for twenty years—and, after all, it was only fair that they should, for had not Pyotr Nikolaevich Lebedev been the first man to detect the pressure of sunlight, back at the very beginning of the twentieth century? But they had never succeeded.

And they would never stop trying. Dimitri was up to something—and it would be spectacular.

Aboard the official launch, a thousand miles behind the racing yachts, Commodore van Stratten looked at the radiogram with angry dismay. It had traveled more than a hundred million miles, from the chain of solar observatories swinging high above the blazing surface of the Sun; and it brought the worst possible news.

The Commodore—his title was purely honorary, of course; back on Earth he was Professor of Astrophysics at Harvard—had been half expecting it. Never before had the race been arranged so late in the season. There had been many delays; they had gambled—and now, it seemed, they might all lose.

Deep beneath the surface of the Sun, enormous forces were gathering. At any moment the energies of a million hydrogen bombs might burst forth in the awesome explosion known as a solar flare. Climbing at millions of miles an hour, an invisible fireball many times the size of Earth would leap from the Sun and head out across space.

The cloud of electrified gas would probably miss the Earth completely. But if it did not, it would arrive in just over a day. Spaceships could protect themselves, with their shielding and their powerful magnetic screens; but the lightly built solar yachts, with their paper-thin walls, were defenseless against such a menace. The crews would have to be taken off, and the race abandoned.

John Merton knew nothing of this as he brought *Diana* around the Earth for the second time. If all went well, this would be the last circuit, both for him and for the Russians. They had spiraled upward by thousands of miles, gaining energy from the Sun's rays. On this lap, they should escape from earth completely, and head outward on the long run to the Moon. It was a straight race now; *Sunbeam*'s crew had finally withdrawn exhausted, after battling valiantly with their spinning sail for more than a hundred thousand miles.

Merton did not feel tired; he had eaten and slept well, and *Diana* was behaving herself admirably. The autopilot, tensioning the rigging like a busy little spider, kept the great sail trimmed to the Sun more accurately than any human skipper could have. Though by this time the two square miles of plastic sheet must have been riddled by hundreds of micrometeorites, the pinhead-sized punctures had produced no falling off of thrust.

He had only two worries. The first was shroud line number eight, which could no longer be adjusted properly. Without any warning, the reel had jammed; even after all these years of astronautical engineering, bearings sometimes seized up in vacuum. He could neither lengthen nor shorten the line, and would have to navigate as best he could with the others. Luckily, the most difficult maneuvers were over; from now on, *Diana* would have the Sun behind her as she sailed straight down the solar wind. And as the old-time sailors had often said, it was easy to handle a boat when the wind was blowing over your shoulder.

His other worry was *Lebedev,* still dogging his heels three hundred miles astern. The Russian yacht had shown remarkable maneuverability, thanks to the four great panels that could be tilted around the central sail. Her flipovers as she rounded the Earth had been carried out with superb precision. But to gain maneuverability she must have sacrificed speed. You could not have it both ways; in the long, straight haul ahead, Merton should be able to hold his own. Yet he could not be certain of victory until, three or four days from now, *Diana* went flashing past the far side of the Moon.

And then, in the fiftieth hour of the race, just after the end of the second orbit around Earth, Markoff sprang his little surprise.

"Hello, John," he said, casually over the ship-to-ship circuit. "I'd like you to watch this. It should be interesting."

Merton drew himself across to the periscope and turned up the magnification to the limit. There in the field of view, a most improbable sight against the background of the stars, was the glittering Maltese cross of *Lebedev,* very small but very clear. As he watched, the four arms of the cross slowly detached themselves from the central square, and went drifting away, with all their spars and rigging, into space.

Markoff had jettisoned all unnecessary mass, now that he was coming up to escape velocity and need no longer plod patiently around the Earth, gaining momentum on each circuit. From now on, *Lebedev* would be almost unsteerble—but that did not matter; all the tricky navigation lay behind her. It was as if an old-time yachtsman had deliberately thrown away his rudder and heavy keel, knowing that the rest of the race would be straight downwind over a calm sea.

"Congratulations, Dimitri," Merton radioed. "It's a neat trick. But it's not good enough. You can't catch up with me now."

"I've not finished yet," the Russian answered. "There's an

old winter's tale in my country about a sleigh being chased by wolves. To save himself, the driver has to throw off the passengers one by one. Do you see the analogy?"

Merton did, all too well. On this final straight lap, Dimitri no longer needed his copilot. *Lebedev* could really be stripped down for action.

"Alexis won't be very happy about this," Merton replied. "Besides, it's against the rules."

"Alexis isn't happy, but I'm the captain. He'll just have to wait around for ten minutes until the Commodore picks him up. And the regulations say nothing about the size of the crew—*you* should know that."

Merton did not answer; he was too busy doing some hurried calculations, based on what he knew of *Lebedev*'s design. By the time he had finished, he knew that the race was still in doubt. *Lebedev* would be catching up with him at just about the time he hoped to pass the Moon.

But the outcome of the race was already being decided, ninety-two million miles away.

❖

On Solar Observatory Three, far inside the orbit of Mercury, the automatic instruments recorded the whole history of the flare. A hundred million square miles of the Sun's surface exploded in such blue-white fury that, by comparison, the rest of the disc paled to a dull glow. Out of that seething inferno, twisting and turning like a living creature in the magnetic fields of its own creation, soared the electrified plasma of the great flare. Ahead of it, moving at the speed of light, went the warning flash of ultraviolet and X rays. That would reach Earth in eight minutes, and was relatively harmless. Not so the charged atoms that were following behind at their leisurely four million miles an hour—and which, in just over a day, would engulf *Diana, Lebe-*

dev, and their accompanying little fleet in a cloud of lethal radiation.

The Commodore left his decision to the last possible minute. Even when the jet of plasma had been tracked past the orbit of Venus, there was a chance that it might miss the Earth. But when it was less than four hours away, and had already been picked up by the Moon-based radar network, he knew that there was no hope. All solar sailing was over, for the next five or six years—until the Sun was quiet again.

A great sigh of disappointment swept across the solar system. *Diana* and *Lebedev* were halfway between earth and Moon, running neck and neck—and now no one would ever know which was the better boat. The enthusiasts would argue the result for years; history would merely record: "Race canceled owing to solar storm."

When John Merton received the order, he felt a bitterness he had not known since childhood. Across the years, sharp and clear, came the memory of his tenth birthday. He had been promised an exact scale model of the famous spaceship *Morning Star,* and for weeks had been planning how he would assemble it, where he would hang it in his bedroom. And then, at the last moment, his father had broken the news: "I'm sorry, John—it cost too much money. Maybe next year . . ."

Half a century and a successful lifetime later, he was a heartbroken boy again.

For a moment, he thought of disobeying the Commodore. Suppose he sailed on, ignoring the warning? Even if the race was abandoned, he could make a crossing to the Moon that would stand in the record books for generations.

But that would be worse than stupidity; it would be suicide—and a very unpleasant form of suicide. He had seen men die of radiation poisoning, when the magnetic shielding of their ships had failed in deep space. No—nothing was worth that. . . .

He felt as sorry for Dimitri Markoff as for himself. They had both wanted to win, and now victory would go to neither. No man could argue with the Sun in one of its rages, even though he might ride upon its beams to the edge of space.

Only fifty miles astern now, the Commodore's launch was drawing alongside *Lebedev,* preparing to take off her skipper. There went the silver sail, as Dimitri—with feelings that he would share—cut the rigging. The tiny capsule would be taken back to Earth, perhaps to be used again; but a sail was spread for one voyage only.

He could press the jettison button now, and save his rescuers a few minutes of time. But he could not do it; he wanted to stay aboard to the very end, on the little boat that had been for so long a part of his dreams and his life. The great sail was spread now at right angles to the Sun, exerting its utmost thrust. Long ago, it had torn him clear of Earth, and *Diana* was still gaining speed.

Then, out of nowhere, beyond all doubt or hesitation, he knew what must be done. For the last time, he sat down before the computer that had navigated him halfway to the Moon.

When he had finished, he packed the log and his few personal belongings. Clumsily, for he was out of practice, and it was not an easy job to do by oneself, he climbed into the emergency survival suit. He was just sealing the helmet when the Commodore's voice called over the radio.

"We'll be alongside in five minutes, Captain. Please cut your sail, so we won't foul it."

John Merton, first and last skipper of the sun yacht *Diana,* hesitated a moment. He looked for the last time around the tiny cabin, with its shining instruments and its neatly arranged controls, now all locked in their final positions. Then he said into the microphone: "I'm abandoning ship. Take your time to pick me up. *Diana* can look after herself."

There was no reply from the Commodore, and for that he was grateful. Professor van Stratten would have guessed what was happening—and would know that, in these final moments, he wished to be left alone.

He did not bother to exhaust the air lock, and the rush of escaping gas blew him gently out into space. The thrust he gave her then was his last gift to *Diana*. She dwindled away from him, sail glittering splendidly in the sunlight that would be hers for centuries to come. Two days from now she would flash past the Moon; but the Moon, like the Earth, could never catch her. Without his mass to slow her down, she would gain two thousand miles an hour in every day of sailing. In a month, she would be traveling faster than any ship that man had ever built.

As the Sun's rays weakened with distance, so her acceleration would fall. But even at the orbit of Mars, she would be gaining a thousand miles an hour in every day. Long before then, she would be moving too swiftly for the Sun itself to hold her. Faster than a comet had ever streaked in from the stars, she would be heading out into the abyss.

The glare of rockets, only a few miles away, caught Merton's eye. The launch was approaching to pick him up—at thousands of times the acceleration that *Diana* could ever attain. But its engines could burn for a few minutes only, before they exhausted their fuel—while *Diana* would still be gaining speed, driven outward by the Sun's eternal fires, for ages yet to come.

"Good-by, little ship," said John Merton. "I wonder what eyes will see you next, how many thousand years from now?"

At last he felt peace, as the blunt torpedo of the launch

nosed up beside him. He would never win the race to the Moon; but this would be the first of all man's ships to set sail on the long journey to the stars.

May 1963